I0518976

STAND AND DELIVER YOUR HEART

Barbara Cartland

Barbara Cartland Ebooks Ltd

This edition © 2020

ISBNs

9781788674201 EPUB

9781788674218 PAPERBACK

Book design by M-Y Books

m-ybooks.co.uk

THE BARBARA CARTLAND ETERNAL COLLECTION

The Barbara Cartland Eternal Collection is the unique opportunity to collect all five hundred of the timeless beautiful romantic novels written by the world's most celebrated and enduring romantic author.

Named the Eternal Collection because Barbara's inspiring stories of pure love, just the same as love itself, the books will be published on the internet at the rate of four titles per month until all five hundred are available.

The Eternal Collection, classic pure romance available worldwide for all time .

THE LATE DAME BARBARA CARTLAND

Barbara Cartland, who sadly died in May 2000 at the grand age of ninety eight, remains one of the world's most famous romantic novelists. With worldwide sales of over one billion, her outstanding 723 books have been translated into thirty six different languages, to be enjoyed by readers of romance globally.

Writing her first book 'Jigsaw' at the age of 21, Barbara became an immediate bestseller. Building upon this initial success, she wrote continuously throughout her life, producing bestsellers for an astonishing 76 years. In addition to Barbara Cartland's legion of fans in the UK and across Europe, her books have always been immensely popular in the USA. In 1976 she achieved the unprecedented feat of having books at numbers 1 & 2 in the prestigious B. Dalton Bookseller bestsellers list.

Although she is often referred to as the 'Queen of Romance', Barbara Cartland also wrote several historical biographies, six autobiographies and numerous theatrical plays as well as books on life, love, health and cookery. Becoming one of Britain's most popular media personalities and dressed in her trademark pink, Barbara spoke on radio and television about social and political issues, as well as making many public appearances.

In 1991 she became a Dame of the Order of the British Empire for her contribution to literature and her work for humanitarian and charitable causes.

Known for her glamour, style, and vitality Barbara Cartland became a legend in her own lifetime. Best remembered for her wonderful romantic novels and loved by millions of readers worldwide, her books remain treasured for their heroic heroes, plucky heroines and traditional values. But above all, it was Barbara Cartland's overriding belief in the positive power of love to help, heal and improve the quality of life for everyone that made her truly unique.

AUTHOR'S NOTE

It was in the eighteenth century that the highwayman became the greatest menace so that no main road was safe for a traveller.

But he was also thought to be a romantic.

In actual fact, however, few of them were anything but the very worst type of criminal, who would murder or torture their victims.

There were, as I have told in this novel, a few wellborn highwaymen, who came from much respected families and had been educated at public schools.

William Parsons was a Baronet's son, who was educated at Eton and was commissioned in the Royal Navy.

Simon Clarke was a Baronet in his own right but became a highwayman.

They behaved much better than Dick Turpin, the most romanticised of all highwaymen, who was both brutal and unscrupulous.

Some highwaymen escaped the gallows, but the majority were hanged at Tyburn, which, until the end of the eighteenth century, was the most uncivilised sight. Tyburn was where Marble Arch is now situated and close to Hyde Park.

There would be thousands in the crowd assembled to witness the hangings with the gentry sitting in the expensive seats, which were close to the gallows.

The mob, who could not afford the closest view, fought fiercely for the best places.

Spectators often had their limbs broken and some were even killed in the crush.

Apart from this, Tyburn was a well known fairground with sideshows and street vendors offering their wares.

In 1789 the gallows were moved from Tyburn to the courtyard of the Old Bailey.

But a hanging was still open to the public and matters were not very much improved.

CHAPTER ONE
1817

Vanda rode through the woods thinking that it was the loveliest day they had had for a long time.

There were primroses and violets peeping through their leaves under the trees and the birds were singing sweetly.

She always enjoyed being able to ride in the great Park that encircled Wyn Hall.

Mr. Rushman had been the manager of the estate during the War with the French.

He had given her permission to go there whenever she liked as he knew how much she enjoyed every moment that she was on a horse.

The old Earl of Wynstock was bedridden and his son was fighting against Napoleon in the Peninsula.

"It would be very nice to see someone young about the place," Mr. Rushman had said, "and there will be no need for you to take a groom with you."

That to Vanda was more important than anything.

Her father had insisted that she was accompanied at all times when she rode elsewhere from her home.

They lived on the border of Wyn Park at the end of the village in the pretty and charming Manor House.

She had really only to cross the road under the trees to be, as she told herself, totally free.

She was thinking that it would be very frustrating now that the War was over and, when the Earl did return, she could no longer use his extensive grounds as if they were her own.

The young Earl, whom she used to play with as a child, had come into the title just three years ago.

He had distinguished himself at the Battle of Waterloo and received the medal for gallantry. He had then joined the Duke of Wellington's staff in Paris to serve him in the Army of Occupation of France.

Soldiers were being demobilised and thousands began to return to England.

There was no sign, however, of the Earl.

'Perhaps he will never come back,' Vanda thought to herself happily.

She rode on towards the centre of the wood where she knew no one but herself ever went.

There, closely surrounded by trees, were the remains of an ancient Chapel.

It had once been used by a monk, who retired from the world to minister to the countryside birds and wild animals.

He was a very Holy man and there were many sorts of legends in the County of the animals he had healed.

Foxes, which had been caught in a trap, would have died had he not placed his hands on them. Cats and dogs that were injured and birds with a broken wing or leg were taken to him usually by children.

He prayed over them and gave them his healing touch.

They left, so the legends said, stronger and healthier than they had ever been before.

The tiny Chapel he had built for himself had fallen into disrepair and the villagers believed he haunted the wood and were afraid to go there by day or at night time.

"How can you be afraid," Vanda asked one old woman, "of someone who was so Holy and who loved the animals and birds so much?"

"He were Holy right enough," she answered, "but it be creepy-like a-seein' he's dead."

No one in the village would ever put a single foot inside Monk's Wood, however often they went in the other woods.

Vanda knew only too well that some of the boys went there to poach And she thought personally that they did very little harm.

With the Earl and his gamekeepers now away at the War, there was no one to shoot the pheasants and pigeons.

Nor for that matter the magpies and jays as well, which the gamekeepers thought of as vermin.

For Vanda the woods were therefore very much more enjoyable. She loved being alone so that no one could disturb her.

She loved listening to the buzz of the bees, the rustle of the rabbits in the undergrowth and the chattering of the red squirrels searching for nuts.

Sometimes too she thought that she could hear music that came from the trees themselves.

She tried to compose it into a music file that she could play on the piano.

Her mother had been an exceptionally good pianist and Vanda had tried to emulate her since she was a child.

She was thinking now that she should compose a song of spring and she was convinced that the trees were giving her inspiration.

The wind moving through the green leaves was creating a melody that she must try to remember.

Then suddenly she heard a strange sound.

It interrupted her thoughts and somehow seemed alien and coarse in all the beauty around her.

There was another sound and she drew in her horse.

Her father was always proud that he kept exceedingly good horseflesh in his stable and the stallion that Vanda was riding was called *Kingfisher* and he was her favourite.

Kingfisher responded at once to her pull on the reins and came to an abrupt standstill.

Vanda realised that straight ahead in the very centre of the woods, where she had never seen anybody before, there were men.

The sound she had heard was a coarse laugh.

Now listening intently she could hear their voices and she knew immediately that they did not belong to any local men.

The inhabitants of Little Stock, as the local village was named, spoke with a slow but distinct Wiltshire accent.

Sometimes she laughed with her father at what they said and the way they spoke. But she thought actually that it was quite attractive.

Whoever they might be ahead of her in the wood were talking harshly to each other.

Their accent was quite different and there was something about the sound of their voices that she did not like.

In fact she felt unaccountably afraid,

Who, she then asked herself, could possibly be making so much noise in the one place in the wood that many people thought of as Holy?

She supposed that they must be some village hooligans, but from which village?

How dare they trespass in the private estate of the Earl of Wynstock?

These were unanswerable questions and she knew that it would be a mistake to try to find out the answer.

The laughter came again and then the chatter of coarse voices.

She could not understand what was being said, but she was sure that there were three or perhaps more men speaking.

She turned *Kingfisher* round and went back along the moss-covered path by which she had come.

When she could no longer hear the odd sounds behind her, she felt angry that the strictest privacy of the wood was being violated by unseemly strangers.

She wondered just what they could be doing there in the wood and why they found it so amusing.

'I shall never know the answers to those questions,' she told herself. 'But I do hope they will go away and never come back.'

It suddenly struck her that they might do damage to the great house itself.

Wyn Hall was a magnificent example of the work of the Adam Brothers. It had been completed in the middle of the previous century on the site of a much older house.

The Earls of Wynstock dated back to King Henry VIII.

They had grown more important down the centuries and each one had improved the house that they lived in and they had also bought more land.

Having been brought up in the shadow of the great Wyn Hall, Vanda had a deep affection for it.

In the same way she loved the old Earl.

He was a distinguished man who enjoyed the company of her father, who was nearly the same age as he was.

The Earl had never been in the Army, but he liked to hear of the life that Vanda's father, General Sir Alexander Charlton, had lived.

He told him about the many years he had spent with his Regiment in India and how well it was doing under British rule.

When the Earl died, Vanda knew that her father felt lost without him.

He had been shattered by her mother's death and, when she was no longer there, he was just like a man who had been crippled.

He was, however, able to forget his unhappiness when he had a friend of his own age to talk to.

Now she thought sadly that he only had her.

Although she tried very hard to fill the gap in his life, it was difficult to do anything but listen when he talked on and on endlessly about his long life.

Fortunately 'the General' as the village liked to call him, was now writing a book and it was taking him a long time because he had so much to remember and so much to record.

At least, Vanda thought now, he must have reached the year when she was born.

She was certain that when it was finished it would be of great interest to the public.

She in fact had had considerable difficulty in persuading her father to write down the stories he told so amusingly.

Her mother had loved them all hugely even though she had heard them told hundreds of time

"Then tell Vanda," she would plead with him, "how you quelled a mutiny among your sepoys."

Or else she would say,

"Describe the real beauty of the Palace belonging to the Maharajah of Udaipur and the pink one you liked the best in Jaipur."

Vanda adored her father's tales.

She knew that the task of writing his reminiscences was making all the difference to his life.

He had been writing when she had left the house and he would not realise how many hours she had been away.

It was only for the last eighteen months that he had been unable to accompany her on horseback.

At first she felt guilty, knowing how much he enjoyed being on one of his well-bred horses.

Sir Alexander's legs were swollen with rheumatism and it hurt to walk let alone ride.

Vanda now reached the end of the wood.

She wondered if she should go home and tell her father about the strange men in the centre of it.

Then she had a better idea.

She would ride up to The Hall and tell the caretakers to be on their guard.

If the hooligans were really intent on making trouble, they might stone the windows of the house or perhaps try to break some of the stone statues in the garden.

'I will warn the Taylors, the caretakers of the house,' she decided.

She rode *Kingfisher* quickly through the Park under the ancient oak trees, across the bridge that spanned the lake and straight into the stables.

She was so used to going there that it was almost like coming home.

As she then reached the yard, the Head Groom, who had known her since she was a child, came out of the stable.

He smiled a greeting before he said,

"Afternoon, Miss Vanda, it be a sight for sore eyes to see thee."

"Thank you. I hope you are feeling better and that the cut on your hand has healed, Repton," Vanda replied.

"It 'ealed immediate after you tells me what to do with it," the Head Groom replied.

He took *Kingfisher* from her and led him into a stall.

Vanda walked along the path through the big banks of rhododendrons which led to the kitchen door.

She did not knock, but went along the flagged passage to the kitchen.

It was a very large room with a high ceiling. There was a large beam on which they had hung game and dried hams in the past.

Now there was nothing on the beam but one small rabbit.

The caretakers were sitting at a large deal table drinking tea.

Taylor would have risen when Vanda appeared, but she said quickly,

"Don't move, I only came in for a moment or two to tell you something."

"Now sit you doon, Miss Vanda. Mrs. Taylor said, who was a large and rosy-cheeked woman. "I'm sure you could do with a cup of tea and Taylor and me were a-just havin' one."

"I would love a nice cup of tea," Vanda replied.

She knew that it was what they expected to hear.

Although she did not really enjoy the strong dark Ceylon Tea they always drank, they would have been disappointed if she had refused a cup.

When it had been poured out and the cup was beside her, Vanda began her story,

"Such a strange thing has just happened. I was riding in Monk's Wood and what do you think was right in the centre where no one ever goes except myself? There were men!"

She paused for a short moment.

Then, as Mr. and Mrs. Taylor did not speak, she went on,

"They were all strangers and they most certainly did not come from Wiltshire. There were quite a number of them too and laughing in what I thought was an unpleasant manner."

It was then that she was aware that Mr. and Mrs. Taylor were looking at each other.

She felt, although it just seemed incredible, they were not surprised at what she had said to them.

"They be in Monk's Wood?" Taylor asked at last very slowly. "Now what on earth do you think that they'd be doin' there, Mother?"

He looked at his wife as he spoke.

She did not answer, but seemed to be busying herself pouring out more tea into her cup. Although it was already nearly full.

Vanda looked from one to the other and then she asked them,

"Have you heard of these men before?"

"No, no," Mrs. Taylor answered quickly. "We knows nothin' about 'em."

She was obviously becoming agitated and so spoke in a way that was not in the least like her.

Vanda next looked at Taylor.

She did not speak, but he was well aware that she was asking him a question,

"I knows of nothin' we can tell you, Miss Vanda," he said at length. "They 'as nothin' to do with us."

"But you are aware they exist," Vanda insisted. "Have they been here causing any trouble?"

Mrs. Taylor put down the teapot and laid her two hands palm down on the table as she turned to say to Vanda,

"Now just you listen to me, Miss Vanda. Go home and say nothin' of what you've heard. There be nought you can do about it and we wants no trouble."

"Trouble?" Vanda asked in a bewildered tone. "What sort of trouble are you talking about and how can it possibly affect you?"

Mrs. Taylor looked helplessly at her husband.

"We be alone 'ere, Miss Vanda," he said, "except for the grooms and Repton be an old man while Nat and Ben be high on a horse but small on the ground."

Vanda would have smiled at the description of the two younger grooms, who did in fact look rather like jockeys, if she had not been feeling so worried.

'What can be going on?' she wondered. 'And why are the Taylors being so mysterious about it?'

When she then thought about it, there was really no one to tell.

Mr. Rushman, the Manager, was over seventy and could no longer ride a horse on the estate, but instead drove a gig.

He was not in good health and in the winter was laid up with bronchitis and rheumatism, which kept him in his house week after week.

She pulled her chair nearer to the table and, resting her chin on her hands she said,

"Now tell me what it is that is troubling you both. You know I will help if I can and, if you want me to remain silent, I will say nothing to anybody."

Taylor looked at his wife.

Mrs. Taylor let out a big sigh that seemed to shake her whole fat body.

"We'll tell you," she offered at length, "but I for one be too afraid to even speak of them."

"Speak of who?" Vanda asked.

Taylor cleared his throat,

"It be like this, Miss Vanda. We be 'ere as you knows to look after the 'ouse till 'is Lordship comes back 'ome."

"No one could do it better," Vanda said encouragingly.

It was true that, with the help of three women from the village, the house was as well looked after as when the old Earl was alive.

Granted there were not four footmen in the hall as had been usual or a butler in charge of them.

Nor was there a chef in the kitchen, the equal of the one employed by the Prince Regent and with four scullions under him.

When the Earl had died, Mr. Rushman had appointed the Taylors as caretakers of the house.

They had certainly lived up to that name and had taken the greatest care of Wyn Hall and they had always in the past told Vanda how much they enjoyed their job.

She just could not understand what could have occurred now to make them so frightened and reluctant to talk of their fears.

"Go on," she prompted Taylor.

"They comes 'ere first about two weeks ago," he began,

"They?" Vanda asked. "Who are *they*?"

"That be what we ain't supposed to know," he replied, "but they be men."

Vanda knew that from the voices she had heard so she did not interrupt and Taylor continued,

"They asks for water and they says to the Missus and I, 'you keep your eyes to yourselves and your lips closed and no harm'll come to you'."

"They said that!" Vanda exclaimed. "And what did you reply?"

"They be not the sort of men you'd make any reply to," Taylor said.

"Then what happened."

"Don't tell 'er, don't you tell 'er," Mrs. Taylor said in an agitated manner.

"I had much better know the whole truth," Vanda said, "and then if anything happens I will be able to help you."

"Nothin'll happen, but nothin'." Mrs. Taylor chimed in. "They promised that if we said naught."

"I don't count," Vanda said with an encouraging smile, "and I don't like to see you both so upset."

"We be upset right enough," Taylor said, "but there be nothin' we can do about it. Nothin'!"

"So where are these men?" Vanda asked.

There was a pause.

Then lowering his voice to little more than a whisper Taylor informed her,

"They be in the West wing, Miss Vanda."

Vanda looked at in astonishment.

The West wing had been shut up for a long time before the old Earl had died. He had decided that the house was too big and the West wing had a good number of rooms that were never used.

In the East wing there was the fine Picture Gallery, the ballroom and a few bedrooms on the top floor and the West wing was just some rooms of no particular historical interest.

Vanda thought that the architects had built it merely to balance from the outside the other wing of the house. At the same time it was definitely a part of Wyn Hall.

She could not imagine anything more horrifying than having hooligans, or whatever these strangers were, living in the house.

It seemed extraordinary that the Taylors had not gone to see Mr. Rushman and demanded that these men were turned out.

She knew, however, that it would be a mistake for her to criticise their behaviour in any way.

She therefore said,

"If they have threatened you, then it must have been very frightening. But surely they don't intend to stay for long."

"We don't knows about that," Mrs. Taylor replied. "We just keeps ourselves to ourselves and pretend that they ain't there."

"But they are trespassing," Vanda pointed out quietly.

"We knows that," Taylor said, "but they are dangerous, Miss Vanda, and we 'ears tales of things that 'ave 'appened, which might 'appen 'ere."

"What sort of things?" Vanda enquired.

Again he lowered his voice so she could hardly hear and she was really reading the movements of his lips as he said,

"Murders."

"I don't believe it!" Vanda exclaimed. "And if these men are murderers, then how can we allow them to be here in The Hall and near the village?"

Taylor glanced over his shoulder because he was afraid that they were being overheard.

"Not so loud, Miss Vanda," he begged her. "If anythin' 'appens to thee we'd ne'er forgive ourselves."

"No indeed," Mrs. Taylor agreed at once. "Now you say nothin' aboot it, Miss Vanda, and perhaps they'll go away."

"And if they stay?" Vanda asked.

The Taylors looked at each other and she realised how frightened they really were and she wondered what she could say to comfort them.

At the same time she was trying to decide quickly who could turn out these trespassers.

They had taken possession of an empty house with no one to protect it but two elderly people.

'I suppose,' she thought, 'it would be foolish to believe that something like this could never happen especially after a war.'

Men after risking their lives in fighting for their country had been turned out of the Services without a pension. Even those soldiers who had been wounded or had lost a limb had been granted no compensation.

Her father had been informed of what was happening in the coastal areas.

Sailors who had been dismissed from the Navy roamed the countryside in search of food and demanded money from quite humble householders.

"I can hardly blame them," Sir Alexander had remarked bitterly. "They won the War, but no one is concerned about them now that there is peace."

"Surely the Government should do something," Vanda had suggested hotly.

"They should," her father had replied, "but then I doubt if they will."

They had gone on to talk about how the men who had fought came back to find that their jobs had been taken by those who had stayed at home.

Many men in battle were lost altogether and could never be traced

Now that hostilities had ended there was no longer the desperate requirement for food that there had been over the last fifteen years.

And farmers could not now sell their crops in an open market.

Also a great many aristocratic landowners had suffered financially from the War.

They could not employ the large numbers of staff they had been able to do before it began.

Tenants needed their houses repaired, but the landlords did not have the necessary money to spend on doing it.

It was so difficult to know exactly where England could find purchasers of what goods there were available for sale.

'There must be somebody who could make these men behave,' Vanda was thinking.

She felt she could hear again the sharpness of the voices and the rough way they spoke in the wood.

But she knew that there were few men available in the village who could stand up to them.

Finally she decided that it was something that she must discuss with her father as soon as she could.

He would know if there was any Military in the vicinity.

If the worst came to the worst, they could get soldiers to turn out the intruders who were causing trouble.

'That is what I must do,' she mused.

But equally she knew that it would be a mistake to tell the Taylors what she was intending to do about this serious problem.

"I can see you have been very brave," she said gently, "but at the same time it is something that cannot continue."

"Now don't you be doin' anythin' about this yourself, Miss Vanda," Taylor said hastily. "If you do, they might 'urt thee and the General."

"I doubt that," Vanda answered. "They can hardly come into the village, bursting into people's houses and beating up or murdering ordinary citizens."

"That's exactly what these men will do," Taylor said stubbornly.

Vanda stared at him.

"Now you are a sensible man, Taylor," she said, "and you know as well as I do that we cannot have rough people taking the law into their own hands in this County."

"This lot," Taylor remarked with the jerk of his thumb, "be above the law."

Vanda shook her head.

"Nobody is above the law and no one has the right to interfere with or to threaten ordinary citizens – "

"You don't understand," Mrs. Taylor interrupted.

She looked at her husband and went on,

"You'd better tell who they be."

"It'd be a mistake," Taylor replied sharply.

Then he added,

"Well, as Miss Vanda knows so much, she 'ad better understand that unless she keeps 'er lips closed we'll be in bad trouble."

Again Vanda was staring from one to another.

She was trying to understand exactly why they were so frightened and why they were so determined that she should do nothing.

She was suddenly afraid that these men might break into the rest of the house.

Wyn Hall was so beautiful inside and she felt as if every piece of furniture and every picture and all the books in the great library belonged in some way to herself.

She had known and loved them ever since she was old enough to appreciate such exquisite possessions.

Wyn Hall had definitely become as familiar to her as her own house and she knew that, if any of it was damaged, it would break her heart.

Now she thought with horror of the miniatures that hung on the walls in the drawing room.

The portraits of the Wyns that hung on the beautifully carved stairs and the pictures in the Gallery, which had been added to by every Earl.

She clasped her hands together.

"We must protect The Hall from these terrible people," she asserted. "Supposing they ransack the State rooms and supposing they set the whole place on fire?"

"They'll not do that, Miss Vanda," Taylor said, "so long as we give 'em shelter. But if we tries to then turn 'em out anythin' might 'appen."

"They cannot stay here indefinitely," Vanda persisted.

"They'll go when it suits 'em," Taylor said. "They just want somewhere to rest and 'ide their 'aul."

"Hide their haul?" Vanda repeated. "What do you mean by that? What can they have to hide?"

They were questions that once again seemed to leave the Taylors silent and fearful.

In fact Vanda began to think it was ridiculous. Taylor was a well-built man. Why should he be shaking in his shoes when he thought about a few riotous young men who so far had done no harm as far as she knew?

"Now what I want you to let me do," she said in a soft voice, "is to talk to my father. You know how clever he is and he has been a soldier all his life."

Mrs. Taylor suddenly gave a scream.

"Soldiers!" she cried. "If soldiers come here they'll kill us. We'll both be dead, that's what we'll be, Miss Vanda, and it'll be you who's done it."

Vanda reached out to put her hand on Mrs. Taylor's

"Please don't upset yourself," she said. "The soldiers will not come here if it frightens you, I can assure you of that, but we have to do something."

"There be nothin' we can do and that be the very truth," Taylor insisted.

"Just you go away and forget us," his wife begged. "We be all right so long as we do nothin'."

Vanda felt as if she was up against an insurmountable obstacle.

After a moment she suggested,

"Tell me where these men come from and who they are. Surely you must know that."

"Yes, we knows that," Mrs. Taylor said in a whisper.

"Then tell me so that I can understand why you are so frightened," Vanda pleaded.

She looked at Taylor.

Again he glanced over his shoulder towards the door as if he thought someone might come through it at any moment.

He then leant across the table and admitted,

"They be 'ighwaymen!"

CHAPTER TWO

Riding home, Vanda wondered what she could do about the Taylors.

They were obviously terrified of the highwaymen.

They had begged her almost on their knees not to tell anyone about them. Nor to try to remove them from the West wing.

And thinking over what she knew about highwaymen, Vanda could understand their fear.

She had often made her father tell her about the terrible menace highwaymen had been when he was a young man.

The most famed of the highwaymen were a fraternity called the 'Knights of the High Toby'.

A number of them, Hawkins, Maclean, Rann and Page had all been in Liveried service.

They therefore modelled themselves on their erstwhile Masters and liked to be thought of as 'the gentlemen of the road'.

There were also, Sir Alexander had said, some men who actually were gentlemen and had found it the only way to earn money.

"It must have been very dangerous, Papa," Vanda had commented.

"They nearly all of them ended up on the gibbet," her father related.

"Were there real gentlemen who would do anything so outrageous?" Vanda enquired.

Her father thought before he responded to her question,

"Maclean was of good Highland stock and his father was a Minister and then William Parsons was a Baronet's son, educated at Eton and Commissioned in the Royal Navy."

"How could they have sunk so low," Vanda exclaimed.

"Sir Simon Clarke was a Baronet in his own right," her father continued.

"It seems incredible that they should do anything which would make them outlawed completely from Society."

"They certainly were," Sir Alexander smiled. "But some of them retained the manners of their class."

"Who in particular?" Vanda enquired,

"James Maclean did deserve the title of a 'Gentleman Highwayman,'" Sir Alexander replied. "He accidently fired his pistol and wounded the famous Horace Walpole in Hyde Park."

Vanda was surprised, but she did not say anything and her father went on,

"He was profoundly sorry and so sent Mr. Walpole two letters of regret."

"He at least was a decent sort of man," Vanda remarked.

"There were unfortunately a great many who were the exact opposite," Sir Alexander stated.

He thought for a moment before he carried on,

"Perhaps two of the worst were Captain James Campbell and Sir John Johnson, who abducted an heiress. She was only thirteen, but had been heir to a fortune of more than fifty thousand pounds."

"What happened?" Vanda asked.

"They compelled her to marry James Campbell against her will."

"How terrible for her."

"It was," Sir Alexander said grimly. "Sir John Johnson was hanged for his part in the abduction, but James Campbell escaped to the Continent."

Thinking of these stories now, Vanda wondered what sort of men they were living in the West wing.

From what she had heard of their voices they might be as murderous and as terrifying as the Taylors believed them to be. On the other hand they might be led by someone better born and not so violent.

'Perhaps I am just being optimistic,' she reflected.

They had most certainly appeared very ferocious to the Taylors.

As she drew nearer her home, she decided that she must tell her father what was happening and she must swear him to secrecy.

But she was quite sure that, however horrified he might be by this new situation, there was nothing that he personally could do about it.

Suddenly it occurred to her that if the highwaymen were just as overpowering as they were reputed to be, she and her father could also be in danger.

Theirs was the largest house in the village and from a highwayman's point of view, they were certainly wealthy.

Against a really determined gang of armed men, they had no defence whatsoever.

Besides her father and herself, there were in the house only Dobson and Jennie who acted as butler and cook. Also Hawkins, who had been her father's batman.

Although he was getting on in age, he was indispensable.

Two women came in to do the cleaning in the house four times a week.

But at night, now she thought of it, with the exception of herself everyone in the house was old.

'If I don't tell Papa, whom can I tell?' she asked herself.

She felt that she on her own was carrying too heavy a burden and, having gained the confidence of the Taylors, she must try to help them in some way if she possibly could.

The real difficulty was how to do so.

She took her horse to the stable where the two grooms, both over fifty, were looking after her father's horses. They took *Kingfisher* from her and led him into his stall.

Vanda walked slowly and thoughtfully back to the house.

She was still undecided.

At the same time every instinct told her that she could not sit back complaisantly and hope that the highwaymen would just go away.

'I must discuss it all with Papa,' she decided finally.

She walked into the study and to her surprise her father was not at his desk. Instead he was seated in one of the more comfortable armchairs in front of the fireplace.

There was a book that he had obviously been researching on his knees and he was lying back with his eyes closed and Vanda realised that he had fallen asleep.

She stood in the same place for a moment just looking at him.

Although he was still an exceedingly distinguished and good-looking man, he was beginning to show his age.

His hair was almost white and in repose there were lines from his lips to his chin that she did not remember noticing before.

'I cannot upset him,' she thought. 'It would be unkind. I shall have to think this problem out for myself.'

She went very quietly out of the room closing the door behind her.

Then she remembered Mr. Rushman. After all he was in the exalted job of the Manager of the Wyn estate.

Although he too was old, in his position he could take action to preserve his Master's house.

Now she thought about it, she was very certain that Mr. Rushman could make an appeal to the Lord Lieutenant.

Alternatively he could write to the Officer in charge of the Army Barracks, which were not far away at Melksham.

'That is the solution,' Vanda told herself triumphantly.

She knew that she must go to Mr. Rushman at once.

There was no need to ask for *Kingfisher* again as Mr. Rushman's house was inside the wall that encircled the Park and she could walk there in under ten minutes.

Without bothering to change from her riding habit, she went out of the front door and ran down the stone steps.

She then entered the Park through the side gate that she had always used

Hurrying along under the oak trees she came in sight of The White Lodge.

It was not really a lodge, but had replaced one that had guarded a different entrance to the Park many years ago.

The lodge had become a very attractive and comfortable house and Mr. Rushman had lived in it with his wife since he was first appointed Manager of the estate by the old Earl.

Now his wife had died and he was living there alone.

Yet he seemed to be quite happy and there were always a great number of callers at The White Lodge.

There were the villagers with grievances over a leaking roof or a broken window and there was a number of people like the doctor, the Vicar and Members of the local Hunt who looked on Mr. Rushman as a friend.

The General was very fond of him and so was Vanda.

She thought that she had been unnecessarily foolish in not at once realising that she should have gone straight to Mr. Rushman.

Also she should have advised the Taylors that was what they should have done.

Mr. Rushman's housekeeper, who was a very superior middle-aged woman, opened the door.

"It's so nice to see you, Miss Charlton, and I'm sure Mr. Rushman'll be delighted to see you."

She hurried across the hall without waiting for Vanda's reply.

Only when she reached the door into the Estate Office where Mr. Rushman usually worked, did she turn to say in a whisper,

"His legs are hurting him today and it's all the worse for because, as he'll tell you it himself, something important is happening."

"Important?"

Vanda longed to question her, but the housekeeper had already opened the door.

"Miss Charlton to see you, sir," she announced.

Vanda walked in.

Mr. Rushman was not at his desk, but sitting upright in a high-backed armchair with his legs raised on a stool.

He had a number of papers and account books arranged beside him. And he was writing with a large quill pen.

He looked up and smiled as Vanda walked towards him.

"You are just the person I want to see, Miss Vanda," he said, "and actually I was just going to send a message to your father."

"What about?" Vanda asked as she sat down in a chair near him.

"I have news," Mr. Rushman said, "good news. But at the same time it would come at a time when it is difficult for me to move."

"And what is your good news?" Vanda enquired.

Mr. Rushman replied almost dramatically,

"His Lordship, the Earl, is coming home!"

*

The Earl of Wynstock arrived in London.

It was such a long time since he had been in England and everything in his view had changed.

Not, he thought, for the better.

The streets were more crowded and there appeared to be a great number more beggars than he remembered.

He had not missed after landing at Dover the numbers of demobilised soldiers and sailors who were to be seen in every town where he had stopped. They were lounging about with obviously nothing to do.

Or, in many cases, sitting despondent by the roadside, hoping against hope that somebody would take pity on them.

The Earl had already heard, while he was still in France, that this was happening in England.

Now he saw it for himself, it made him very angry.

After fighting for five long years against Bonaparte, no one appreciated more than he the courage and the endurance of the British soldier.

He had heard the same story from his friends who had been in the Royal Navy.

It seemed to him just appalling that the men who had served under Admiral Nelson and the Duke of Wellington and had saved bravely England in the War should be treated so shabbily.

He was determined that he would speak about it as soon as he had the opportunity in the House of Lords.

He was, however, aware that there would be a great deal for him to do once he had arrived home.

First he must open Wyn House in Berkeley Square and then Wyn Hall in Wiltshire.

The Duke of Wellington thought that the Earl was one of the most able of his Officers in that he was a great genius for organisation.

The Earl was sensible enough to be aware that this was something he would certainly need in reconstructing his own life.

At twenty-nine so many of his years had been concerned with war and he knew that it would be difficult to readjust to a very different existence.

He had, in point of fact, found the many gaieties of Paris almost overwhelming after the hardship and the danger of the battlefields.

He had gone to Paris with the Duke of Wellington from Cambrai, where the Army of Occupation was billeted.

He had felt at first dazzled by the notorious extravagant and fascinating *courtesans*.

He was amazed by the way that the French had adjusted themselves overnight to peace after the defeat of Napoleon Bonaparte.

Paris was once again the City of pleasure and the Earl would have been inhuman if, when he was off duty, he had not enjoyed it.

He indulged himself in several exhilarating and fiery affairs with the most sophisticated and experienced women in Europe.

Then he became involved with Lady Caroline Standish.

She was beautiful, exotic and had stalked him, as if he was a stag, from the first moment she set eyes on him.

A widow since the age of twenty-one, she had made the most of being related to a number of the greatest aristocratic families in England.

It was influence that had enabled her to reach Paris very shortly after hostilities had ceased.

Because she was rich, the parties that she gave for every attractive man in the British Army were much sought after and they rivalled even those given by and for the *courtesans*.

The Earl was not quite certain how it happened, but he found that Lady Caroline was with him wherever he went.

Without meaning to he then met her practically every day and it was on her insistence that it became every night.

It was only when it was almost too late that he realised that she was seeking not only amusement but marriage.

One thing he had determined during the War was not to get married until he was very much older and ready to start a family.

He had heard too much, not only from his close friends but also from the men he commanded, of unfaithful wives.

"I trusted her," a brother Officer told him bitterly, "not only with my house, all my money and my children but also with my heart."

He went on to tell the Earl exactly what had happened to him. It was inevitably one of his relatives who had informed him in the first place of his wife's infidelity.

Because the Earl was a good Officer and his men trusted him implicitly, he learnt about their troubles as well.

"Gone off with the innkeeper without tellin' me she 'as," his Sergeant-Major told him, "and my mother writes to tell me 'er 'as stripped the 'ouse of everythin' I bought for it."

There were innumerable men who had been cuckolded by their closest friends, besides even the carrier, the landlord or the gamekeeper.

It was then that the Earl began to wonder if all women were untrustworthy.

He felt that a woman who took lover after lover was not a particularly admirable specimen of her sex.

He had never known his mother, whom he had adored, being concerned with any man except his father.

He told himself that, when he did get married, it would be to someone who would love him and him alone. And he would kill his wife rather than share her with another man.

He would, however, have been totally inhuman if he had resisted Lady Caroline's experienced blandishments.

She entwined herself around him like clinging ivy.

It was only when there was talk of him returning home that he realised he stood on the brink of a very dangerous gulf.

"I hope I shall be able to get away next month," he had said to Caroline.

They were having dinner in the house that he had rented with another brother Officer while they were in Paris.

It was a bore to have to stay at the British Embassy with the Duke of Wellington.

Hotels were practically non-existent and uncomfortable and sordid.

The house his friend had found had belonged to one of Napoleon's many social upstarts, who had been disdainfully ignored by the French of the *Ancien Régime*.

It was expensively furnished and fairly comfortable and

the servants who were in charge of it were delighted to have regular wages from two Englishmen who paid punctiliously.

The Earl's friend was seldom in the house and he found himself continually having dinner alone with Lady Caroline.

He had to admit that she looked very alluring.

As the daughter of the Duke of Hull, she had taken London by storm the moment she appeared as a *debutante*.

She had made a good marriage in marrying a man who came from a family that was as blue-blooded as her own and he was also extremely rich.

When he was killed in a tragic carriage accident, it did not perturb her unduly.

She had already found him dull and before he was dead she had amused herself with several lovers.

Caroline Standish was wise enough to appreciate that her beauty would not last forever.

Her limitless extravagance both in England and France had considerably eaten into her fortune and she was therefore looking for a husband who was both rich and distinguished.

Who better than the Earl?

Her golden hair gleamed in the candle light. Her gown, which was in the high-waisted style, originally started by the Empress Josephine, was very revealing.

After the announcement that he would be going home, the Earl said casually,

"Will you be staying here?"

Lady Carolines's large blue eyes then looked up at him in surprise.

"Surely, Neil," she said softly, "you know that I will be coming with you."

The Earl stiffened.

He had found Caroline extremely attractive.

But he had no intention of arriving in London with her as part of his baggage.

He knew that not only his houses were waiting for him but his family too.

He was well aware of just how much she would shock his grandmother, aunts, cousins and all their friends.

There was silence.

Then Caroline said in a low seductive voice,

"I love you and if I cannot live without you, I am quite certain you cannot live without me."

The Earl thought that it was not the sort of conversation one should have at the dinner table.

When he had taken Caroline back to her house, he had very unwisely, he thought later, stayed with her as he usually did.

She had been far too experienced to continue with this conversation, which she was aware had been a shock to the Earl.

Instead she used every wile she knew of to arouse his passion.

As she was very experienced and he was very much a man, it was not a difficult thing to do.

Later they were lying closely in the large, canopied bed and there was only a very faint light from a cupid-fashioned candelabrum behind the curtains.

Caroline drew a little nearer.

"How could anyone," she asked the Earl, "have a more wonderful lover? My darling, we shall be very very happy together."

The Earl, who was practically asleep, became suddenly aware of the danger. He had been aware of it in the same way when he was on the battlefield.

He knew that Caroline had chosen this moment when he was at his weakest to press her suit on him.

With an effort he yawned.

"I must go back," he said. "The Duke wants me to have breakfast with him."

Caroline's hands were touching him and her lips were very close to his.

"I want you to stay with me," she whispered. "I find it hard to lose you even for what is left of the night."

The Earl abruptly climbed out of the bed.

"One thing I really dislike," he said conversationally, "is having to discuss political strategy at breakfast."

"You are not listening to me," Caroline said petulantly.

"I am sorry," the Earl replied, "but I really am tired."

He dressed quickly whilst Caroline watched him.

Lying back against the pillows, she looked as beautiful as a translucent pearl in a velvet-lined box.

The Earl then moved as fast as he could manage towards the door.

"Goodnight, Caroline."

She gave a little cry of protest.

"You have not kissed me goodnight! How can you be so cruel?"

He stopped before he reached the door as she stretched out her white arms seductively

The Earl was well aware this could be a trap that had caught many men unawares. If Caroline was to put her arms round his neck, he would lose his balance.

He would fall on top of her, which was exactly what she wanted.

He took her hands and kissed first one and then the other.

"Thank you for making me so happy," he murmured.

Even as she cried out in a last attempt to prevent him from going, he closed the door behind him.

His carriage was waiting outside and he drove back to his own house where he was staying.

He was wondering frantically how he could avoid being married to Caroline Standish and he was prepared to admit that it was his own stupidity that had made him so involved.

Already and this was, of course, engineered by Caroline, people were beginning to link their names together in Paris.

And doubtless the gossips were also talking about them in London as well.

Too late he saw that he should have prevented her from being always at his side and, of course, from then talking to all and sundry.

What woman did not talk?

Caroline was clever enough to use public opinion when it suited her.

When he finally climbed wearily into his own bed, he was still asking desperately exactly what he should do and the question turned over and over in his mind.

His valet called him early the next morning and after a cold bath he dressed himself in his uniform and hurried to the British Embassy.

To his considerable relief he was alone at breakfast with the Duke.

They discussed several propositions that had come from the French as the British were now doing everything in their power to reduce the overall size of the Army of Occupation and send back home as many soldiers as was possible.

Suddenly the Earl had an idea.

"I am wondering, Your Grace, if you would consider sending me back to London as soon as practical."

The great man looked at him penetratingly.

The Earl was aware that he knew that he had an ulterior motive in this request.

"You want to go home?" the Duke asked.

"If it is possible for you to spare me, Your Grace."

The Duke considered this request for a moment or two and then he said,

"I shall miss you, of course, I shall miss you."

He smiled and went on,

"But I appreciate, Wynstock, that you could easily have refused to stay with me this last year having an unanswerable excuse in the necessity of attending to your own affairs."

The Earl inclined his head and the Duke continued,

"I think I can guess your reason for wishing to be gone and, if you will take my advice, you will leave without fond farewells, recriminations or tears."

With a slight twist of his lips, the Earl knew that this was what the Duke often suffered himself.

Aloud he answered,

"That is extremely kind of Your Grace. If I can do as you say, it will make everything a great deal easier."

"Very well," he replied. "I order you to go tomorrow."

"Thank you," the Earl murmured.

"I will give you certain letters for the Prime Minister," the Duke said shortly, "and, as they are, of course secret, you can arrange your leaving so that no one will be aware of your departure until you have gone."

"Thank you, thank you a thousand times," the Earl said again.

It was all much easier than he had anticipated. Keeping secrets from the French had been drummed into the members of the Duke of Wellington's Staff.

As one wit put it,

"I am now afraid of my own shadow."

The Earl dined with Caroline and fortunately there were a number of other men present.

She was at her very best, holding everyone spellbound by her charm and wit.

She flirted outrageously with every man from the oldest to the youngest.

It was, the Earl appreciated, a glittering performance.

He was certain from the way she looked at him under her eyelashes and pouted her lips provocatively that it was acted done for him.

She was demonstrating just how she could entertain his friends and, if she could shine against an alien background, how much better at Wyn Hall?

Caroline had once been to Wyn Hall with her father and had never forgotten it.

The Earl was fully aware that more than anything else in the world she wanted to become its chatelaine and to sit at the end of his table wearing the famous Wynstock jewels.

He left the party at nearly one o'clock and he knew that Caroline was perturbed that he did not stay until the rest of her guests had gone.

"I have to be up early," he told her truthfully.

He was aware that she thought that it was only a parade.

Or that once again he was breakfasting with the Duke of Wellington.

"Come to me as soon as you are free," she whispered to him and her eyes told him exactly what that meant.

When their relationship had first started, he had found her exciting to the point when it was hard to think of anything else.

He had on several occasions, at her invitation of course, called on her in the morning. She was certainly alluring with her golden hair falling over her naked shoulders.

She usually wore little except a necklace of emeralds or one of black pearls that enhanced the whiteness of her skin.

The Earl did not pretend for a moment that he had not been infatuated with her.

But an *affaire de coeur* was one thing and marriage was another.

He could not imagine in any way his wife, the Countess of Wynstock, receiving a man into her bedroom at night time while the servants sniggered about it downstairs.

As he left Paris for Calais, he knew that he was running away.

However he told himself that it was a wise General who knew how to withdraw in the face of superior odds.

He would live to fight another day!

As soon as he had arrived in London, the Earl found that there were a thousand things for him to do.

He took the secret papers to the Prime Minister.

The Earl of Liverpool wanted to hear a great deal about the Army of Occupation that was not in the reports that he had received.

The Earl then decided he must call on the Prince Regent and, if he did not do so, he would certainly be in the Black Book at Carlton House.

The Prince Regent was certainly delighted to see him.

The Earl was new and so very interesting, something that His Royal Highness was always seeking.

He insisted on his lunching, dining and meeting with his many friends and even mere acquaintances.

He asked the Earl to accompany him to a Race Meeting at Epsom, to a meal on Wimbledon Common and to a display of swordsmanship at Gentleman Jackson's gymnasium.

In between these activities, the Earl engaged servants to run his house in Berkeley Square for him.

He also bought a number of fine horses at Tattersalls sale rooms.

Invitations poured into Wyn House as soon as the great Social Hostesses of London realised that he was back.

There were, of course, also a number of old friends to meet at White's Club and they too had suggestions for what he should see and who he should meet.

They told him about the pretty new ballerinas at *Covent Garden* and the pleasures of *The White House*, which he had not enjoyed before he had gone abroad.

And actually who were the latest Incomparables whom he would be very stupid to ignore.

It was rather like Paris, but at the same time he found the Prince Regent witty and undoubtedly amusing.

The *soirées* and Receptions were somewhat dull. The Incomparables not so fantastic or so fiery as Caroline.

Even to think of Caroline made him wonder if he had really escaped or if she would follow him back to England.

When he had heard nothing for nearly a week now, he thought optimistically that she had found Paris too exciting to leave.

Then, as he walked into Whites, he instantly saw one of his closest friends, who said to him,

"I have just been told that a good friend of yours is back in London."

The way he spoke and the expression in his eyes made the Earl draw in his breath.

"Who are you talking about?" he asked.

There was no need to listen to the answer.

"Caroline Standish."

The Earl instantly made up his mind.

'I will go to the country,' he told himself, 'and I will leave first thing tomorrow morning.'

CHAPTER THREE

Vanda stared at Mr. Rushman in some surprise before she exclaimed,

"The Earl is coming home? When?"

Mr. Rushman glanced down at a letter beside him.

"His Lordship says," he replied, "that he will be leaving London on Wednesday, which is actually today. That means he should be here on Friday."

Vanda made a little murmur before he went on,

"His Lordship asks that I send a pair of the best horses to *The Dog and Duck* at Gresbury."

He looked at Vanda and added,

"You do know, Miss Vanda, as well as I do that we have nothing in the stable that his Lordship would consider worth driving."

Vanda knew that this was true.

When the old Earl died, the horses were already getting on in years and gradually most of them were put out to grass in the paddocks. And what remained were only useful for the grooms to ride to the village to collect provisions.

She saw the worry in his face and said quickly,

"I know that Papa would be delighted to send a pair of our horses to carry the Earl on the last leg of his journey."

"That would be extremely kind of you," Mr. Rushman replied, "as I am sure that his Lordship wishes to arrive with a flourish."

He smiled as he spoke.

Vanda had the idea that he was thinking of the Earl as they had last seen him.

A young man of twenty-two, full of enthusiasm and a magnificent rider.

"There are indeed a great many other things to do," Mr. Rushman went on, "for I expect his Lordship has forgotten that the house has been closed and the staff either dismissed or retired."

"Buxton is living in the village," Vanda volunteered.

She was thinking of the butler who had always been a very impressive pontifical figure at Wyn Hall.

In the past the whole house seemed to revolve around him.

"I have remembered that," Mr. Rushman pointed out, "and thank goodness Mrs. Medway is alive."

"Do you think they will come back?" Vanda asked.

"I am sure that they will if you beg them to do so," Mr. Rushman replied. "They will at least be willing to oblige us until we can employ younger people to take their place."

"Me?" Vanda enquired. "You want me to ask them?"

Mr. Rushman made an eloquent gesture with his hands.

"When I had received this note from a groom who had ridden post haste from London, I was wondering who would help me and how I could reach Buxton and Mrs. Medway."

He paused before he added,

"I can, of course, try to crawl there myself!"

"You know I will do anything you want," Vanda said, "and it will be very exciting to have Wyn Hall full again and the Earl in charge."

"I am afraid that things are not like they used to be," Mr. Rushman said sadly, "but the Taylors have done their best."

Vanda realised that in the excitement of hearing about the Earl's return she had for a moment forgotten the Taylors.

And in particular the reason why she had called on Mr. Rushman.

Knowing just how much he had on his mind, she felt that she could not add to his many difficulties.

After all she thought to herself, if the highwaymen now refused to leave, there was nothing that he personally could do about it.

The Earl was returning and so it would be up to him to protect his own property.

She rose to her feet.

"I will go now and talk to Buxton and Mrs. Medway. I would suppose that they can employ anyone they wish from the village."

"Everyone on two legs as far as I am concerned," Mr. Rushman replied. "I can only pray that the house is not as dusty as I fear it may be."

"Don't worry about it," Vanda said. "The Taylors have been wonderful and the women who clean the rooms every week have kept it looking exactly as it did when the Earl's father was alive."

Mr. Rushman gave a sigh of relief.

"That is one burden off my mind, Miss Vanda."

Vanda smiled,

"Dare I ask you," he continued, "to see if Mrs. Jacobs is capable of taking over the kitchen until I can find a chef."

"She is very old," Vanda answered, "but she could sit down and tell the others how things should be done."

She considered for a moment and then went on,

"Mrs. Taylor is quite a good cook and there are several women in the village who could help them."

"You are an angel from Heaven when I was almost in despair," Mr. Rushman declared.

"I expect that is where I would get my reward," Vanda laughed. "I will go off and see these three important people concerned with his Lordship's comfort and then report to you later what they say."

"Thank you, *thank you*," Mr. Rushman cried. "And tell your father also how grateful I am."

Vanda hurried away.

She knew better than anyone else how much there was to do.

If The Hall was to be made comfortable and the Earl as well served as he remembered, they needed time.

She was only a little girl of ten when, after he had left Oxford University, he had gone into the Horse Guards.

It was always known as the family Regiment.

He had come home, perhaps twice the following year. Then he left England and no one had seen him again.

He had, of course, written to his father who showed the letters to Sir Alexander.

Both of them recognised that the young Viscount, as he was then, would be in the thick of the fighting.

When there were so many casualties reported back from the battlefields of Europe, it seemed almost a miracle, Vanda thought, that he had survived.

Yet he had and she knew that he would be horrified if he returned to find the house still closed up, the Taylors almost incoherent with fear and highwaymen in the West wing.

Whilst Vanda was thinking all these thoughts, she had been walking quickly towards, the village.

She soon came to a small attractive cottage that Buxton, the butler, had been retired to and it was, of course, one of the many cottages that belonged to the Wyn estate. It was in good repair and had been recently painted.

The garden was bright with spring flowers.

As she walked slowly up the path to the front door, she wondered if Buxton would feel too old to do what was asked of him.

He opened the door.

She thought at once, although his hair was dead white, that he looked in good health.

"This be a surprise, Miss Vanda," he said, "but a very pleasant one. Will you please come in?"

"Thank you, Buxton," Vanda smiled.

She walked into a small room that was the kitchen and where Buxton habitually sat.

On the other side of the entrance passage there was a very small parlour. It was kept for important occasions and could hold no more than four people.

Vanda, because she knew that Buxton would expect it, sat down in an armchair in front of the stove.

"I have good news for you," she said. "His Lordship has returned to England and will be arriving home on Friday."

"Friday!" Buxton exclaimed.

"Yes," Vanda answered, "and Mr. Rushman, who is too ill to come and see you himself, has asked me to beg you to get the house ready for him."

She was watching the old butler as she spoke.

For a second she thought that he was going to refuse. Then, as he smiled, she thought that there was a light in his eyes that had not been there before.

"Be Mr. Rushman giving me a free hand, Miss Vanda?" he enquired.

"You can have anybody and everything you may want," Vanda assured him. "And you know just as well as I do that nobody could make the place ready but you."

"Very well, Miss Vanda, I'll do my best," Buxton said, "but I'll need a lot of help."

"Mr. Rushman's actual words were that you could have 'everyone on two legs'," Vanda replied.

Buxton laughed.

She knew that she had won this particular battle at any rate.

Almost the same conversation next took place in Mrs. Medway's cottage, which was identical to Buxton's.

But being a women she still needed rather more coaxing and, of course, more flattery.

"Who else but you," Vanda asked, "would know what sheets to put on the beds and make sure that they are properly aired?"

She paused before she added,

"What is more, if you say 'no', I think Mr. Rushman will worry himself into an early grave."

"Well, I'll surely do what I can," Mrs. Medway said at last rather reluctantly. "I'm too old now to cope with them young girls who think they know better than I do."

This was an old cry that had echoed down the ages and

Vanda agreed with her that the young were uppish and not as respectful as they should be.

By the time she left, Mrs. Medway was calculating who in the village she would need to help her.

Vanda knew that with Buxton and Mrs. Medway at The Hall in their old positions then the Earl would be comfortable from the moment when he arrived.

Then she had seen Mrs. Jacobs,

She agreed to go to The Hall if she could be taken there in a carriage as her legs were not as good as they had been.

It was only as Vanda walked home that the problem of the highwaymen returned to her mind.

She wondered again what she should do about it.

Then just before she reached her own home, she recalled a frightening story that her father had told her many years ago.

A highwayman, who she thought was called 'Watson', had tortured a diamond merchant into giving over more than half his fortune.

Watson and his accomplice had captured the merchant when he was returning to his house on the outskirts of the City of London. Then they took him forcibly to an empty barn in the countryside.

There they forced him at knife and pistol point to write them a cheque for many thousands of pounds and because Watson could make himself look quite presentable, the Bank had handed over the money without querying the size of the sum involved.

They had then decamped, leaving their prisoner tied up and helpless in an isolated spot.

It was only by an extremely lucky chance that he had been discovered by some passing children. He was alive, but practically dead from starvation.

The tortures he endured affected his health to the point that he died two years later.

Both the highwaymen had been caught and hanged for theft and Vanda now remembered hearing that story among a number of others and thought that it was all very frightening.

She had forgotten these stories until this moment and she wondered if the same treatment could possibly happen to the Earl.

Granted that there would be a good number of servants in The Hall and their arrival might drive the highwaymen away.

Yet as well as being in the house, the Earl would want to ride all over the estate. He could hardly do so with enough grooms to outnumber the highwaymen.

She thought now that she had been rather remiss in not asking the Taylors how many of them there were. However they were likely to have seen only two or three of them at any one time.

There might be any number of others with them in the West wing as well.

'The Earl could be riding into a ghastly trap,' she told herself and wondered what she could do about it.

She had now reached The Manor House.

She went first to the stables where she found the two old grooms.

She told them that they were to take her father's two best carriage horses to *The Dog and Duck* at Gresbury.

The grooms were obviously pleased.

"Our 'orses will need exercise, Miss Vanda," the senior groom said.

"We's exercised them as you know," the other chimed in, "but we were only sayin' the other day they be gettin' fat, and a fat 'orse's a lazy 'orse."

"I am sure, as his Lordship wants to get home quickly, when you put them between the shafts at Gresbury, they will have to stretch themselves."

"That's what'll be good for 'em," the groom replied.

Vanda ran into the house.

Her father was working away on his book and he was delighted to hear the news about the Earl's imminent return.

"I was wondering only the other day when that young man would be coming home," he said. "I shall look forward to talking to him."

"It will be all about the War!" Vanda protested. "You do know, Papa, that there is a great deal for the Earl to do on the estate and the farmers have been asking for a long time when he will be back."

"Neil was always a good young man," Sir Alexander said, "and he will prove to be an excellent soldier. I have no fears for the future."

Vanda wished that she could say the same thing.

After they had finished dinner, she said 'goodnight' to her father, kissed him on his cheek and went upstairs to bed.

Alone she asked herself again how she could warn the Earl about the highwaymen in his house and what he would do about them.

It would certainly be foolhardy for him to confront them personally.

She supposed that he would think the right thing to do would be to contact the Barracks.

He could ask for soldiers to arrest the highwaymen for trespassing on his estate.

She then had the frightened feeling that this might end in a shooting match. If it did, undoubtedly some men would be wounded if not killed.

Then she thought that the highwaymen would hardly be so foolish as to stay in the West wing.

As soon as they were aware that there was a great deal of activity in The Hall itself, they would leave.

This meant that they might take to the woods, especially Monk's Wood, where she had first heard them.

Then the story of the diamond merchant returned to her mind and once again she felt sure that the Earl was running into danger.

'There is only one thing I can do,' she decided finally, 'And that is to warn him before he reaches home.'

She wondered why she had not thought of that before.

If the horses were going to Gresbury, so could she. And the grooms would take them tomorrow, so that they would have a good night's rest at *The Dog and Duck* before the Earl drove them home to The Hall.

If she left on Friday morning as soon as it was dawn on *Kingfisher*, she could be at the inn by breakfast time and well before the Earl left.

She thought it over carefully.

She then decided, in case she missed him, she would ride along the side of the road for the last five miles and he could not then pass her without her seeing him.

Early the following morning, she went up to The Hall to see what was happening.

She found Mrs. Taylor trying to organise what seemed to be almost an army of women. They had arrived from the village all together on Mrs. Medway's instructions and they were all gossiping excitedly needless to say about the Earl.

Vanda knew as soon as she moved among them that the Taylors had not mentioned the highwaymen to them.

She walked round the different rooms.

Now the shutters were open, the windows cleaned and the sunshine seeping in made the house look lovely.

She found Taylor alone in the larder sorting out the food that was coming in from the farms.

Two young lambs, half a dozen fat ducks, a dozen or so chickens and a mountain of eggs!

In a low voice, just in case someone might be listening, Vanda asked,

"Have they – gone?"

There was no need to explain who she meant.

"They be there last night, Miss Vanda," Taylor said in a conspiratorial tone.

When Vanda left him she walked to the back of the West wing, moving silently through overgrown rhododendrons.

The lower windows were shuttered and she stood outside one in the centre of the wing that belonged to the principal sitting room.

She listened intently, thinking that if anyone moved or talked inside she was bound to hear them.

There was no sound and she prayed that the highwaymen had taken the hint and had gone.

She was not really sure if that would make things better or worse.

If they were in the woods waiting for the Earl to appear, what chance would he have against armed men?

She went home more determined than ever that she must warn him before he could reach The Hall.

Perhaps he would change his mind and then go back to London. Alternatively he might go first to the Barracks for assistance.

She could not bear to anticipate what his reaction would be and yet she knew that she would be doing the right thing in warning him so that he was at least prepared.

Sir Alexander talked about the Earl and his family all through luncheon.

He was so delighted to have lent him his horses and he then he reminisced about his friendship with the old Earl and the issues that they had discussed when he was alive.

She thought that the Earl had been extremely sensible in deciding to stay the last night of his journey at a Posting inn.

It would have spoilt the excitement of the homecoming if he had arrived late in the day.

However it made it more difficult for her to reach him.

She felt exceedingly guilty in keeping her knowledge of the highwaymen secret. But then what could her father or Mr. Rushman do themselves without help?

The answer was nothing and she therefore felt that she was entirely justified in tackling the problem on her own.

'If I save the Earl, they will all agree that I have done the right thing,' she told herself.

Then she sent up a little prayer to God for help in this dire situation that she found herself thrust into.

*

The Earl found that it was not as easy to leave London quickly and secretly on Wednesday as he had intended.

He had planned to leave for the country after breakfast.

He was, however, woken up to be told that there was a message for him from the Prime Minister.

It was far too urgent and authoritative to be ignored.

The Earl of Liverpool wished him to explain personally to several members of the Cabinet the latest demands of the French regarding the Army of Occupation.

Also to tell them of the Duke of Wellington's decision to send home ten thousand men.

It was impossible for the Earl to refuse such a request.

He therefore went straight to Downing Street and hoping that he would not have to stay long.

He was over-optimistic.

The meeting went on until well after luncheontime and it was impossible to refuse to eat with the Prime Minister.

By the time he returned to Berkeley Square he knew that he would have to postpone his departure until the following day.

It was annoying, but there was nothing that he could do about it.

He therefore went to White's to find, as he had expected, several of his friends there enjoying themselves.

"Are you going to the Devonshire's tonight?" one asked him. "It is only a small ball but I always enjoy anything that is arranged by the Duchess."

"I have not made up my mind," he replied evasively.

"Then someone will be most disappointed," his friend answered pointedly, "because you are sitting next to her at Carlton House."

The Earl now remembered somewhat belatedly that the Prince Regent had invited him to dine with him before the Devonshire's ball.

He had accepted and he decided that it was an invitation that he must now refuse.

Caroline would most surely contrive in her usual way to make people around them aware that he was her property.

To go to Carlton House would only add to the gossip that he knew was becoming increasingly dangerous.

A man could easily be pressured into marriage by social opinion and gossip could easily fetter him in a way that made an escape impossible.

'What can I do?' he asked himself frantically.

He wished now that he had been able to follow his plan of leaving early that morning for Wyn Hall.

He went quickly back to Wyn House from White's and sat down at his desk to write a most apologetic letter to the Prince Regent.

He had, he wrote to him, been suddenly afflicted with an extremely heavy and dangerously infectious cold. It had made it just impossible for him to attend a dinner party.

"I am not only suffering myself," he carried on, "but I should be most remiss if I did infect Your Royal Highness when you have so many calls upon your time."

The Prince Regent was well known for being extremely fussy about his health.

The Earl knew that this would ensure that his refusal to dine would be taken as an unselfish act and not an insult.

He sent a groom with his letter to Carlton House.

He then dined alone, having given orders that he was to be called at six o'clock the next morning.

His phaeton drawn by the best-looking pair of horses he had just bought at Tattersalls was to be ready by half past six.

His valet and the luggage had already gone ahead in a brake and the grooms with four horses had left first thing in the morning for the Posting inn, where he would change his horses.

Travelling with his valet there was a third groom, who was also an excellent cook. And he would see to it that what his Master had to eat was palatable and the brake also carried his own wine.

The Earl felt that he would be arriving at Wyn Hall by luncheontime the next day.

He was woken by the door of his bedroom opening and he thought that it must be a servant coming to call him.

Then, as he half-opened his eyes, he became aware that someone standing right by his bed was lighting the candles in a silver candelabrum.

To his astonishment it was Caroline!

She held a candle in her hand that he thought must have come from one of the sconces in the passage.

"Caroline!" he exclaimed. "Why on earth are you here at this time of night?"

She turned her face to smile at him.

He saw that she was wearing a very elaborate evening gown and a necklace of perfect diamonds.

"When you did not turn up at either Carlton House or at Devonshire House," she answered, "I felt that I had to see you."

The Earl sat up in bed.

"You must be crazy coming here at night. Think what the world will say when they hear about it."

"The only person who knows where I am now," Caroline replied, "is your night-footman."

"And your coachman?"

Caroline shrugged her shoulders.

"They are paid not to talk and what do servants matter?"

The Earl did not reply, but merely looked at her.

"Go away, Caroline," he ordered at last, "and behave yourself. You may do this sort of thing in Paris, but not in London."

"And who is to stop me," she asked rather aggressively.

As she spoke, he realised that she was undoing the back of her gown. And while doing so her eyes were concentrated on his.

"You are now behaving quite abominably, Caroline," he said. "You have no right to come to my house in this way and I insist on your leaving immediately."

Caroline laughed.

It was a happy sound and seemed to echo through the shadows.

Then, as the Earl wondered what he could do to make her behave more sensibly, she made a little movement with her body.

And her gown slithered slowly down onto the floor.

For a moment she just stood there naked and looking in the light of the candles like a Greek statue of Aphrodite.

Her skin was dazzlingly white and her lovely necklace glistened iridescently.

Then before the Earl could speak another word or move she flung herself against him.

Her arms were round his neck, her lips on his and he felt the fiery passion of them seeping through his body.

*

It was nearly dawn before the Earl persuaded Caroline to leave him.

He watched her putting on her gown slowly.

He made no effort to rise himself or escort her down to the front door.

"Will you give me luncheon?" she asked as she tidied her hair in one of the gilt mirrors.

"I am going to the country."

"The country? Then, of course, I will come with you."

"No, Caroline," the Earl replied. "That is impossible."

"Why? You know I am longing to see Wyn Hall."

"I doubt if you would enjoy it, since it has been shut up with only caretakers to look after it since my father died."

"But we will – be together," Caroline countered softly.

"There is a great deal of dust," he went on, "ceilings that are leaking, beds that are damp and, of course, the squeaking of mice to keep you awake."

He knew, as Caroline gave a little cry, that she disliked mice.

"It cannot be as bad as all that," she exclaimed.

"I expect it will be worse. When I have made everything look as it did before I went to the War, then I might consider giving a house party."

Caroline turned to the mirror with her eyes alight.

"A house party! I will be your hostess, darling Neil. That is a splendid idea and we will ask the Prince Regent as one of our guests. He was saying at dinner that it was something he would look forward to."

The Earl stiffened.

He knew what Caroline had intimated when speaking of 'our' guests.

If she had done so to the Prince Regent himself at the party tonight, he would believe at once that their engagement was just about to be announced.

His lips tightened in a hard line.

As if she was suddenly afraid that she had gone too far, Caroline said,

"I did not actually say it to His Royal Highness that we were engaged, but I think he suspects it."

"We are *not* engaged!" the Earl asserted. "As I have already told you, Caroline, I have no intention of marrying until everything I possess is as perfect as I wish it to be."

"And then I will make you the perfect wife," Caroline replied.

She moved towards the door.

"I shall expect to hear from you, darling, before the end of next week. If not, I shall arrive uninvited and, perhaps, bring the Prince Regent with me."

She did not wait for the Earl's reply, but slipped out of the bedroom, closing the door behind her.

He threw himself angrily back against his pillows.

He was asking himself for the hundredth time what he could do about Caroline and she was, the Earl knew, using every possible weapon against him.

He was not certain how he could prevent himself from being annihilated.

To use the Prince Regent as a kind of intermediary on her behalf was, of course, her trump card.

The Prince Regent liked to be in the know and he loved to play 'cupid'.

He might even, if Caroline could charm him and he was feeling generous, easily offer to hold the Wedding Reception at Carlton House.

A Wedding was just the sort of festive occasion that he enjoyed.

The Earl groaned and closed his eyes tightly.

He could just see the claws of the trap, and God knows it was a man trap, closing around him.

It would only be a question of time before he would be captured and imprisoned and there would be no escape.

Caroline would be his wife and her lovers would eat his food, drink his wine and sleep in his bed.

And thinking as they did so that they were fooling him.

'I cannot bear it,' he murmured to himself furiously.

He wished

with all his heart that he was still fighting Napoleon Bonaparte and the War had never ended.

CHAPTER FOUR

Sir Alexander went into his study.

Vanda walked over to the stables to speak to the grooms before they left for Gresbury.

She knew that they would take the horses slowly and she calculated that if they left at about one thirty, they would be there soon after five o'clock.

They would go cross-country as the journey took much longer by road as there were so many narrow twisting lanes.

The horses were ready, looking well-groomed and, she thought, outstanding enough to please the most fastidious horse-lover.

She remembered how well the Earl had ridden as a boy.

Although she was very much younger than he was, she used to watch him admiringly and she had a strong feeling that, when he did arrive home, he would be only too glad to borrow her father's horses.

That was until he had filled his stables with his own.

The grooms touched their forelocks respectfully.

"We be just off, Miss Vanda, and we've got a letter from Mr. Rushman to 'and to 'is Lordship."

"Don't lose it," Vanda smiled.

"We just 'eard a strange thing, miss," the other groom chimed in.

Vanda turned towards him to listen and he said, "The boy as works in the garden of White Lodge tells us that early this mornin' 'e sees seven men on 'orseback goin' into Monk's Wood."

Vanda was suddenly very still.

She knew only too well who the horsemen were.

She thought that she had been very stupid as she had not remembered when she was thinking about the highwaymen in the West wing that they would have horses.

This meant that they must have stabled them at The Hall.

There were a large number of empty stalls because the stables had been built to hold at least fifty horses.

Now she knew, and she had not suspected it before, that the grooms also had been terrorised just as the Taylors had been.

They had therefore said nothing about the highwaymen to her.

'I should have anticipated this,' she thought.

Furthermore she was horrified at now learning that there were many more highwaymen than she had supposed.

Seven men, all of them fully armed, were a formidable number for any man to encounter.

What would the Earl do about it?

She was aware that the grooms were looking at her and they were obviously surprised by her silence and so she then asked quickly,

"I wonder who the horsemen could be?"

"That's what us bin a-wonderin', Miss Vanda," the older groom said.

"While you are away, I will try to find out if anybody else has actually seen them," Vanda managed to say lightly, "although it seems to me that the boy was dreaming."

"'E be a truthful lad," the groom stood up for him.

He was aware that Vanda was waiting for them to go.

He swung himself into the saddle of one horse and took the leading-rein of the other in his left hand.

"Take them slowly," she advised pointedly.

"We will, Miss Vanda," the other groom replied, "and Jake's lookin' after the other 'orses till we gets back."

Jake was his son and nearly as experienced as his father.

Vanda watched them riding off until they were out of sight.

It was then that she knew that she must give the Earl the information of where the highwaymen were hiding.

She must also give him time to think of what he could do about them.

As she then walked into the house, she realised that if she reached *The Dog and Duck* at Gresbury only in time to pass on her information hurriedly before the Earl drove off on the last stage of his journey, he himself might run into great danger.

The highwaymen might well be planning to hold him to ransom as soon as he arrived at The Hall.

They could easily walk into the house when he was not expecting them.

He would most certainly not be armed and old Buxton and the boys from the village he had taken on as footmen would have no chance of stopping them.

And the women under Mrs. Medway would merely be hysterical and no use to anyone.

By the time Vanda had reached the drawing room she had decided what she should do.

It was very daring and so if anyone knew of it, it would cause a great deal of gossip.

'All that really matters is that the Earl's life is at stake,' she told herself firmly.

She went upstairs to her bedroom and selected just a few things that she would want for the night. She included a light muslin gown that she could change into for dinner.

She rolled them up in a long bag that could be attached to *Kingfisher's* saddle.

She next changed into her best riding habit, which was a very attractive one.

Then, carrying the bag and her riding hat, she went down the stairs.

She laid them down on a chair in the hall.

Then slowly, because she was nervous, she went into her father's study.

Sir Alexander looked up impatiently as he disliked being interrupted.

"I am so sorry to disturb you. Papa," Vanda said, "but I have just had a message from Miss Walters. She is not at all well and I think I should go and visit her."

Miss Walters was an excellent old Governess who had taught Vanda for some years until she retired.

She had a small cottage in a village about a mile from Gresbury and the General knew that Vanda visited her from time to time.

"She is not well?" he exclaimed. "Well, I suppose you will have to go to her, but take Jim with you."

Jim was one of the grooms who had already left.

Vanda knew that her father had forgotten for a moment that the Earl was borrowing his horses.

"I will try to be back before it gets dark," she said. "But if she keeps me too long, I will stay the night."

"I don't like your gallivanting all over the country," Sir Alexander grumbled crossly. "But I would suppose if she has sent for you, there is nothing you can do but help her."

"It would be unkind not to, Papa," Vanda pointed out.

She kissed her father lightly and admonished him,

"Don't work too hard on your book, Papa, and don't forget to take your medicine."

"There is nothing in the whole world wrong with me," the General retorted.

Vanda went from the room.

She knew that, once he was so immersed in his book, he would forget all about her.

Jake saddled *Kingfisher* for her and she set off.

She made a short detour so that she would not encounter the two grooms who in fact by this time would be at least half an hour ahead of her.

They would be aware of how angry her father would be if he knew that she was going such a long way alone.

She had no wish to tell anyone else that there were these highwaymen in the vicinity.

She knew the country that she was riding over so well that she might have been in the Park at Wyn Hall.

She had hunted over this land in the winter frequently and had ridden to Gresbury dozens of times with her father.

It was quite an attractive little village and it boasted one of the few good Posting inns in the County.

So it was not at all surprising that the Earl had arranged to stay there on his way home.

It was a warm sunny day and *Kingfisher* was enjoying the ride as much as she was.

To start with she gave Kingfisher his head and then they settled down to a nice comfortable pace that would ensure that neither of them would be too tired by the time that they reached Gresbury.

They passed by Savernake Forest and it just crossed her mind to wonder if there could be more highwaymen lurking in there.

She so wished that the seven 'gentlemen of the road' in Monk's Wood had preferred the vastness of Savernake to where they were at present.

She was, however, convinced that they would not leave Monk's Wood until they had made a really good haul either in money or valuables from The Hall.

Once again she was thinking with absolute horror of the miniatures, the *objets d'art*, the silver and gold ornaments.

They would all be easy to carry away and would fetch a good sum in a thieves' market.

Without really meaning to she quickened her pace.

It was only just after five o'clock when she turned into the yard of the Posting inn.

An ostler came hurrying towards her and she asked him,

"Have four horses arrived here belonging to General Sir Alexander Charlton?"

"No, ma'am."

"They are not far behind me," Vanda informed him as she dismounted, "and when the grooms arrive they will look after this horse as well."

She inspected the stables and found five stalls that she thought were superior to the others.

She ordered fresh straw for them and then went into the inn.

The landlord, who was a large burly man, bowed to her politely.

"Good day to you, ma'am, and let me welcome you to *The Dog and Duck.*"

"Thank you," Vanda replied. "I have been explaining to your ostler that four horses belonging to my father, General Sir Alexander Charlton, will be arriving very shortly."

The landlord looked suitably impressed as Vanda went on,

"Two of them are for the use of the Earl of Wynstock, who is, I understand, staying here tonight."

"That be right, ma'am," the landlord agreed, "and we're ever so honoured to have his Lordship as our guest."

"As I have a very important message for his Lordship," Vanda said, "I wish to wait until he arrives and so I should be very grateful if you would allow me to do so in your private parlour."

The landlord agreed immediately.

He then took Vanda down a passage that lay behind the public dining room and next he showed her into a small but comfortably furnished parlour where there was a bright fire burning in the grate.

A table by the window was already half-laid for dinner.

Vanda thanked him and asked if she could wash away the dust of her ride.

She was shown upstairs by a mob-capped maid.

Because her hair was slightly blown about by the wind, Vanda took off her hat with its gauze veil.

She carried it in her hand when she went downstairs and

she hoped that the Earl would not be long so that she could ride home before it became really dark.

Otherwise she would have to stay, as she had told her father, with Miss Walters.

That would indeed be rather trying as her old Governess had become very deaf in her old age and almost every word had to be repeated to her several times.

Vanda had found this very exhausting the last time she had seen her.

Nevertheless she had it all well planned.

The important thing was that the Earl should know of the menace that was waiting for him when he arrived home eventually.

*

The Earl awoke and realised that, although it was seven o'clock, he had not been called as he had ordered.

He jumped out of bed and rang the bell furiously.

It was always the same, he thought, when his valet was away his orders were not carried out as precisely as he would wish them to be.

Then he told himself firmly that Croker, who had been his batman in the War, was a soldier and the new servants who had just been engaged had not yet emulated his ways.

A footman came into the room hurrying in response to the bell.

The Earl demanded to know why he had not been called at six o'clock.

"I peeped in, my Lord," the man answered, "and, as your Lordship were sound asleep, I didn't like to trouble you."

The way he spoke and the expression in his eyes told the Earl that he was aware of why he was so tired.

The rest of the household must be well aware of it too.

His lips then tightened into a thin line and he damned Caroline under his breath.

But he realised that it was no use losing his temper and he merely castigated the footman,

"Another time when I say six o'clock, I really *mean* six o'clock!"

"Yes, my Lord."

The footman then helped him to dress.

There was another delay because he was quicker down the stairs than the kitchen had expected him to be.

He had therefore to wait impatiently for his breakfast.

By the time it was all finished and his phaeton brought round from the Mews, it was well after eight o'clock.

The Earl knew that to reach Gresbury that evening, he would have to drive faster than he had intended to do.

It was not that Wyn Hall was too many miles distant from London. It was that the roads, the Earl remembered only too well from the past, were very bad and potholed in most unexpected places.

It was one thing for the Prince Regent to break records when driving to and from Brighton, but quite another to use the twisting narrow lanes which had to be negotiated to reach Wyn Hall.

It was spring and the hedges and the roadside banks of grass beneath them were beautiful with buds, primroses and violets.

The Earl, however, was concentrating on his horses to make sure that he could obtain their best for him.

He was too good a driver to push them too hard and he would certainly take no unnecessary risks.

His horses were excellent and to his relief well-trained.

That was what he had been assured when he had bought them at Tattersalls.

At the same time it was easy when dealing with horses to be deceived and to find, after they were delivered, that the vendor had over-boasted his goods.

The Earl, however, was delighted with his new team.

By this time he knew that they were worth every penny that they had cost him.

He had the good manners to stop by at the posting inn where he had intended to stay the first night. He cancelled his booking, but he generously paid for it.

He had learned when in France to pay for everything the British Army requisitioned from the local inhabitants.

This had astounded the French.

They had never expected to receive so much as a *sou* for the pigs, chickens and ducks they took from the enemy.

"You're a great gentlemen, my Lord." the landlord of the posting inn exclaimed as the Earl put a number of golden guineas down in front of him.

The Earl smiled and then he had driven on.

It was infuriating for one mile to be held up by a farm cart, which it was impossible for him to pass.

It was, however, a very long day, having only stopped halfway to eat a very hurried meal.

He was therefore tired and extremely hungry when he at last turned in at *The Dog and Duck* at a quarter after eight o'clock.

There were two ostlers waiting for him and the landlord was standing in the doorway beaming a welcome.

"You've 'ad a good journey, my Lord?"

"Not too bad," the Earl replied. "Your roads, however, are disgraceful and something ought to be done about them."

"I agrees with your Lordship and every traveller says the same," the landlord replied, "but there be nothin' we can do about it."

The Earl decided that he would certainly make a strong protest to the Lord Lieutenant and he would make it quite clear that there was no reason why the roads should be quite so neglected.

He was sure some of them were completely impassable in winter when there was snow or torrential rain.

He was at this very moment more interested in his own comfort.

The landlord himself took him up to a bedroom, which was the best and largest in the inn.

A small trunk that he had carried on the phaeton was already being unpacked by the groom who had travelled with him.

As he had ordered beforehand, there was a bath ready on the hearthrug in front of the fire.

"Cans of hot water'll be up in a few minutes, my Lord," the landlord said respectfully.

He turned to leave the room.

Then, as if he had suddenly thought of it, he added,

"There be a lady waitin' for your Lordship downstairs. She arrived several hours ago."

The Earl stared at him.

He could hardly believe that Caroline could have got here before him.

"A Lady?" he questioned.

"Miss Charlton, my Lord. The daughter of General Sir Alexander Charlton, whose horses are waitin' here for your Lordship in the stable."

The Earl relaxed at once.

"I understand," he said, "and, of course, I will apologise to the lady for being so much later than I intended. Perhaps she will do me the honour of dining with me."

"I'll tell the lady what your Lordship says."

The landlord went from the room.

The Earl thought that it was in fact a damned nuisance that he should have company at dinner.

It was the last thing that he wanted and he suspected that the daughter of the General would be getting on in years and probably over hearty.

She would be one of those tiresome hard-riding women, who thought they knew more about horses than a man did.

However it seemed that he was borrowing the General's horses for the last segment of his ride back home.

It then struck him for the first time that, if there were any horses left after his father's death, they would be too old to be of much use and also there would have been nobody to order Rushman to buy in new stock.

He was quick-witted enough to understand that in the circumstances Rushman had been astute enough to procure an excellent team from a neighbour.

As he climbed into his bath, the Earl was remembering the General and that he had been a close friend of his father.

'He must be getting on in years by now,' he told himself, 'but his wife was a very pretty woman.'

Then he began to think once again of Caroline and what he should do about her.

She had occupied his thoughts for almost the whole way from London.

He resented that she was spoiling his home-coming to which he had been looking forward with such anticipation.

He felt rather like a small boy who had been deprived of a very exciting present.

He hated Caroline, he told himself.

To be truthful he had known long before he left Paris that she was everything he really disliked in a woman.

At the same time he had been weak enough to be unable to resist the fire that she always aroused in him.

"I have made a fool of myself," he said as he put on his evening clothes.

He took a quick glance at himself in the mirror and then walked down the somewhat rickety oak stairs.

The landlord was waiting for him at the bottom of them.

"Dinner'll be ready in just a few minutes, my Lord," he announced.

"I admit to being very hungry," the Earl replied.

The landlord went ahead of him and he followed him down the oak-panelled passage with its beams overhead into the parlour.

Vanda, who was waiting for him, rose as he entered the room.

When the Earl looked at her, he was astonished.

*

When she had received the Earl's invitation to dine with him, Vanda went and collected her bundle from *Kingfisher's* saddle. She had then been taken up to a bedroom where she could change.

She was glad she had brought an evening gown with her.

It was a very simple one, which she had intended to wear at Miss Walters's house.

Its high waist revealed the curves of her breast and the hem with two simple flounces accentuated the perfection of her slim figure.

She had brought with her no adornments of any kind. But the Earl, looking at her, was thinking that he had never seen hair of such a strangely beautiful colour.

It was very pale and the colour of the dawn when it first appears in the sky.

As if the simile was apt, there were touches of silver-like moonlight amongst the gold.

Because Vanda was so slim her eyes seemed to dominate her face.

They were not the blue that might have been expected with the colour of her hair.

Instead they were green, the green of buds that the Earl had seen in the hedgerows as he drove past them.

There were also little flecks of gold that might well have come from the sunshine.

He had fully expected to see a middle-aged woman, but instead he found himself face to face with a young and very lovely girl.

Suddenly he smiled.

"Now I remember," he exclaimed. "You are Vanda!"

"I thought you would have forgotten me."

"I remember you as a very pretty child who used to ride horses that were far too big for you and swim in the lake like a small fish."

Varda laughed.

"And I have always remembered you taking jumps that your Papa had said disapprovingly were too high for you!"

The Earl chuckled.

"My father said the same thing, but I still tried to make the impossible possible!"

They were both laughing as the landlord hurried in with a bottle of champagne.

Vanda accepted a glass and raised her hand.

"To your home-coming!" she toasted. "We have waited a long time for you."

"I too thought that the years would never pass," the Earl said solemnly.

They sat down at the table to eat and, while the food was plain, it was well cooked.

As the Earl was hungry, he enjoyed every mouthful.

He asked questions and Vanda talked while they ate.

She told him how the house was now in perfect repair and how Buxton and Mrs. Medway had come back to help.

"It may not be in quite as perfect order as it was when your father was alive," she said, "but they are doing their best with very little notice."

The Earl heard the reproachful note in her voice and he answered,

"I know it was inconvenient. At the same time I wanted to leave London at short notice. As it was, I was delayed at the last minute and only left this morning."

"Then you have been travelling all day," she queried.

The Earl nodded.

"You were very lucky. During the cold winter months it sometimes takes three days for anyone to reach us."

Once again the Earl was talking about the roads and the disgraceful state they were in.

The last course was served and the Earl had accepted a glass of delicious brandy.

It was so good that he was certain it had been smuggled.

The servants then withdrew and they were alone.

They moved from the table to sit in the two armchairs in front of the blazing fire. Large logs were burning cheerfully and it was very warm and inviting.

However it was now growing late.

Vanda knew that she must hurry and tell the Earl why she had come to the inn to speak to him.

Otherwise by the time that she reached Miss Walters's cottage, she might be asleep.

"What is worrying you?" the Earl turned and asked her.

"I was thinking that I must speak up quickly, otherwise my old Governess, who lives in the next village and is not expecting me, will not hear me knocking on her door."

"You mean that you are not staying here tonight?"

"Of course not," Vanda said. "I came to see you because it was urgent. If you had not been so late, I had expected to ride home before it was dark."

The Earl looked at her.

Then he asked,

"So why did you have to see me, apart from bringing me your father's horses?"

"They were actually coming without me."

The Earl put down his glass.

"Then what is it that you have to tell me?" he enquired.

He was aware perceptively that, unlike most women, she had not been waiting at the inn for him just for the pleasure of his company.

"Things are happening at Wyn Hall that are exceedingly serious," Vanda began.

She instinctively lowered her voice as she spoke.

The Earl looked at her, but he did not speak.

She then went on,

"It is going to upset you and spoil your home-coming. At the same time I have to warn you and so it is my duty to tell you."

"To warn me?"

"That you may be in grave danger!"

The Earl looked bewildered.

"Why and from whom,"

Vanda drew in her breath.

"For some days now the West wing has been occupied by a band of highwaymen."

The Earl sat upright in his chair and his expression was incredulous.

"Did you say highwaymen? In the West wing? I don't believe it!"

"It is true, my Lord. They have terrorised the Taylors, who are your caretakers and I think, although I have not yet spoken to them, that they have also threatened the grooms."

"So why has no one done anything about it?" the Earl asked surely. "Surely, Rushman – ?"

"Mr. Rushman does not know," Vanda interrupted him. "'Nor does my father. In fact I am the only person, apart from the servants concerned, who knows that they are there."

"It seems to me quite extraordinary that they should go into the house."

"The house has been empty," Vanda pointed out, "and I have been really terrified lest they should ransack the many precious treasures that it contains."

"Why do you think they have not already done so?"

Vanda hesitated and then she thought that the Earl had better hear the truth.

"What I fear," she said, "although I have no foundation for it, is that they need money and intend to extort it from you if you return."

"*If* I return?" the Earl repeated. "Are you then seriously suggesting that I should not do so?"

"I think it might be dangerous, unless you have Military protection."

"I have never heard such ridiculous nonsense!" the Earl said scornfully. "And I can certainly assure you, Vanda, I am not afraid of a couple of highwaymen!"

"There are seven of them," Vanda told him quietly, "and from the terror they have evoked in the Taylors, I think they must be very dangerous men."

"This is certainly something I did not expect," the Earl said. "Do you really think they might injure me?"

"Years ago my Papa told me how a highwayman called 'Watson' extorted a lot of money from a diamond merchant, who subsequently died as a direct result of the rough way that he had been treated."

"I had forgotten that story," the Earl said, "but that was in the last century and actually I did not think of highwaymen being kidnappers."

"Then you have forgotten Captain James Campbell and Sir John Johnson," Vanda replied.

"What did they do?"

"They abducted a girl of thirteen who was an heiress and James Campbell forced her to marry him."

"Good Heavens!" the Earl exclaimed. "Did she escape?"

"The highwaymen were caught and Sir John was hanged but Captain Campbell escaped by going abroad."

The Earl did not speak and Vanda went on,

"I am sure there are just as many highwaymen, robbers and thieves now as there were then, especially with so many men being demobilised without money and without work."

The Earl knew that this was very true and was what he had actually seen for himself.

There was silence until he asked,

"What do you suggest I do?"

Vanda smiled.

"I came to warn you, my Lord, to be prepared not to make decisions for you. After all, you are the soldier."

"At least I knew where my enemy is," the Earl said.

"I told you – at the moment they are in Monk's Wood."

"And you think they will stay there?"

"I cannot be sure, but I think it very likely as they know that you are coming back to The Hall."

"I suppose that is the obvious thing to think," the Earl agreed. "But what can I do?"

"I have already suggested you should go to the Barracks and ask the Officer in Charge to send a Company of men to Wyn Hall."

The Earl considered this for some seconds.

Then he said,

"I suppose, really, I dislike having to admit that I am helpless. Are there no able-bodied men on the estate?"

"There are a few," Vanda admitted, "but most of them, as they have not been in the War, do not know how to shoot and a pitchfork is not very efficient against a bullet."

The Earl slapped his hands down on both the arms of his chair.

"It is just intolerable," he exclaimed. "The situation is as bad as it was fifty years ago. I remember my grandmother telling me that the streets were so dangerous when she was a girl that, when she and her mother moved to and from Court in sedan chairs, they had to be escorted by servants carrying blunderbusses to protect them from robbers."

Vanda laughed.

"At least you can move quicker than that, my Lord."

She paused before she said,

"I cannot but help thinking that if your horses had been better than theirs, they would have taken yours with them."

"I suppose you are right," he agreed rather reluctantly. "But I have to admit it is so humiliating that I cannot protect myself and my staff and I am then obliged to ask help from the Military."

"It would be far more humiliating to be tied up and then forced to give them an enormous sum of money," Vanda said practically.

"That is true. Very well, I will not go straight home, as I had intended, but drive to the Barracks."

Vanda clasped her hands together.

"I am so glad you think that is the sensible thing to do. Now I must go."

She rose to her feet and the Earl berated her,

"Don't be stupid, Vanda. Look at the time."

There was a clock on the mantelpiece and, when Vanda looked at it, she was horrified to find that it was after eleven o'clock.

She stared at it, thinking that it must be incorrect, but the Earl insisted,

"Stay here. I am sure that you are not nervous at being with me."

"No, of course not," Vanda replied. "I am only thinking of my reputation – and of course – yours."

The Earl laughed.

"No one would be surprised to hear I was accompanied by a beautiful lady and you are in fact very beautiful!"

She blushed and he thought that she looked exceedingly lovely as she did so.

"Thank you, my Lord. That is the first compliment that I have had for a long time."

"Is everybody blind in Little Stock?" the Earl enquired.

Vanda's eyes twinkled.

"No, my Lord, they are old."

"I never thought of that," the Earl said. "Of course, all the young men, like myself, must have gone to the War."

"All of them," Vanda said softly. "And some will never come back."

There was a little tremor in her voice.

"Well, you shall have to listen to my compliments," the Earl said, "and as soon as the house is liveable, I will produce my friends from London, who can be far more eloquent than I am."

"Your Lordship is very kind," Vanda replied, "but at the moment I am more concerned with highwaymen."

"If you call me 'my Lord' again, I do think I shall spank you!" the Earl said. "We were brought up together and my name, in case you have forgotten it, is 'Neil'."

"I am well aware of that," Vanda said, "but I thought it would be a mistake to presume on a childhood friendship."

Before he could speak she added,

"No, that is the wrong word – childhood *adoration*. I thought you were all the heroes in the history books, besides undoubtedly being the reincarnation of a Greek God!"

The Earl threw back his head and laughed.

"Until I became the age you are now, I thought that all girls were a nuisance."

As he spoke, he thought that they still were, if they were anything like Caroline.

She was certainly beautiful and yet at this moment he was thinking that Vanda outshone her in a very different way with a beauty that was unique and ethereal.

Aloud he said,

"Now be sensible, Vanda and take a room here for the night. You will have to come with me tomorrow morning to the Barracks to explain just what is now happening at Wyn Hall. As I have never been there, they may not listen to me."

"I think that is most unlikely," Vanda smiled. "Everyone in the County knows how brilliant you have been to the Duke – and the medal you received after the Battle of Waterloo."

"Oh, that!" the Earl exclaimed.

"Yes, that," Vanda then echoed him. "You will find even in peacetime it counts for a great deal."

"Then by the authority I gained during the War," the Earl said, "you will, Vanda, take your orders from me!"

He smiled at her beguilingly and added,

"I will explain to the innkeeper that my being so late has prevented you from going on to where you were staying. And I will inform him that you need one of his best rooms with a maidservant next door in the dressing room."

"I think no one could object to that," Vanda agreed.

"The important thing is for no one to know about it," the Earl remarked. "We will leave early in the morning and, as you suggested, go straight to the Barracks."

He thought for a moment and then he added,

"Perhaps it would be a mistake for us to ride into the village together. We must therefore tell the grooms who will be riding my horses to wait at a place where I can drop you off before I go on to The Hall."

Vanda looked at him approvingly.

"Now you are taking charge!" she said. "And that is just what I wanted you to do."

"And now, as we are both so tired," the Earl suggested, "we will go to bed as soon as I have seen the landlord."

He walked from the room as he spoke.

Vanda felt as if the burden that she had carried on her shoulders since she had spoken to the Taylors at The Hall had lightened.

She was afraid, desperately afraid, that the highwaymen would rob the house of everything in it or injure the Earl.

But at least she had been able to persuade him to ask for assistance.

She was saying a little prayer of thankfulness when he came back into the parlour.

"Everything is arranged," he announced, "so now you can stop worrying about me."

He stood looking at her in a manner that made her raise her eyebrows enquiringly.

"I am wondering how I can thank you," he declared, "for taking such good care of me."

He knew exactly how any other woman he knew would have responded, but Vanda merely said quickly,

"Keep your fingers crossed! We have a long way to go before you are really safe and then I can only go on praying that you will be clever enough to outwit the enemy."

The Earl took her hand in his.

"Thank you so much, Vanda," he said, "I really do need your prayers."

Because he was grateful to her, and also because he had been in France, his lips touched the softness of her skin.

He saw the surprise in her eyes.

He felt the little quiver that went through her body.

CHAPTER FIVE

The Earl came down the stairs for breakfast early to find that Vanda was already in the parlour.

She was looking very smart in her riding habit, wearing a hat that had a gauze veil trailing prettily behind it.

"Good morning, Vanda," he smiled at her. "Now I know you really are a country girl."

"Because I am up so early?" Vanda asked. "I like riding when the world is fresh."

"So do I," the Earl agreed, "and I wish I was riding this morning."

As the landlord and the waitresses came hurrying in with their breakfast, he suggested,

"As I want to talk to you on the way to where we are going, I have told my groom to ride your horse."

He thought Vanda looked as if she was going to refuse and added swiftly,

"He is a very experienced rider and, I promise you, you can trust him."

"I feel sure that I can," Vanda said, "and actually Papa's grooms with your team have already left."

"I thought they would have," the Earl said, "and, if they have to wait for you so that you can ride home with them, I am sure that will present no difficulties."

Vanda had already instructed the grooms to be sure to take the Earl's superlative horses as gently as possible.

They were to meet her at the crossroads.

It was about a mile from the village and she doubted if there would be any people about to notice them.

She well knew that her father, when they arrived home, would be extremely interested in the Earl's new horses.

She thought with a feeling of excitement that it would be wonderful when all the stables at The Hall were again filled with horses to equal or even surpass them.

As they went on with their breakfast, the Earl asked her,

"Did you sleep well?"

"Very well, thanks to you."

There was a question in his eyes and she explained,

"I have been worrying about you riding so blithely into danger. But now that you are going to the Barracks, I am no longer afraid."

"I am just longing to say," he answered, "that the whole situation is exaggerated. I cannot really believe that English highwaymen, however many

~106~

there may be, are anything like as intimidating as the dastardly Napoleon Bonaparte!"

Vanda laughed.

And then she said,

"One is a national problem, the other a personal one."

The Earl liked the quick way she managed to reply to him and he said,

"After what you told me last night about the distressing lack of compliments paid in this part of the country, may I tell you that you look very lovely and very smart."

"You are making me feel as if I was deliberately asking for compliments," Vanda replied, "but now they are here, I am definitely enjoying them."

The Earl laughed.

Vanda could not help feeling that it was very delightful to be with him.

When breakfast was finished, the Earl paid the landlord so generously that he bowed almost right down to the ground in appreciation of what he had received.

Outside the Earl's phaeton was waiting.

When his groom had handed him the reins, he started to move out of the yard.

The groom mounted *Kingfisher* and followed on behind them.

Vanda knew the way to the Barracks, but then the Earl, having been away for so long, was not certain.

He could not go very fast due to the lanes twisting and turning. Or places so tight and narrow that if they met a cart or a wagon one of them would have to go back.

To Vanda's delight the Earl was ready to talk about his experiences in France and best of all he told her how brilliant the Duke of Wellington had been.

"No one else on earth," he asserted positively, "could have succeeded in defeating Bonaparte."

"That is what we all felt," Vanda agreed with him.

"He is the hero of all Europe," the Earl went on, "and when he comes home for good next year, I am only hoping that this country will show him its great appreciation."

"I hope so too," she replied. "He is a very great man."

"And I am so extremely lucky to have been associated with him this last year," the Earl added.

Vanda liked the way he spoke almost humbly about the Duke of Wellington.

The Earl was obviously very reluctant to talk about his own achievements in the War.

After a while the Barracks loomed ahead of them.

She thought sadly that perhaps never again would she have the chance to have such an intimate conversation with the Earl.

They then drove up to the gates and the Earl said who he was and informed the sentry that he wished to speak to the Officer in charge.

"That'll be Major Lawson, sir," the sentry replied.

He pointed the way to the centre building next to the Parade ground and the Earl drove his horses up to it.

There they had to wait until the groom who had been riding *Kingfisher* could find a soldier to hold him.

When he did, the man went to the head of the team and the Earl helped Vanda to alight from the phaeton.

They walked in through an imposing front door with two sentries who came to attention as they did so.

When the Earl again repeated who he was, he was taken immediately to Major Lawson's office.

He was a middle-aged man, looking smart and efficient in his uniform.

He greeted the Earl enthusiastically.

"This is a very great honour, my Lord," he said. "In fact I did not know that you had returned to England."

"I have only just come back," the Earl answered.

"Then I can only say how very glad we are to see you," Major Lawson replied.

"Thank you," the Earl said, "and now may I introduce you to Miss Charlton, who I think you may be aware is the daughter of General Sir Alexander Charlton."

"I don't think we have met," the Major said to Vanda as he shook her hand, "but I know your father and have a great admiration for him."

"Thank you," Vanda smiled.

"We have come to see you on an important matter," the Earl said, "and I should be obliged, Major, if we could talk to you in private."

The Major looked surprised but he agreed at once,

He turned to the young Lieutenant, who was working at another desk in the room and said,

"See that we are not disturbed."

"Very good, sir," the Lieutenant replied.

He then walked from the room closing the door quietly behind him.

The Earl and Vanda then sat down on two chairs near to the Major's desk.

As they did so, Major Lawson asked,

"Now, what can I do for you, my Lord?"

"I think Miss Charlton can explain it better than I could do," the Earl replied.

He looked at Vanda as he spoke who said,

"When I had learned that the Earl was returning to Wyn Hall, I contacted him very early this morning to warn of the danger – "

"The danger?" Major Lawson interrupted in surprise.

"For some time now seven of these highwaymen have been occupying the West wing at The Hall and are terrorising the caretakers and the grooms."

For a moment the Major stared at her in astonishment before he exclaimed,

"So that is where the Baker gang are hanging out!"

"The Baker gang?" the Earl repeated. "Do you mean you have been looking for them?"

"For the last two months," Major Lawson replied. "We were warned by the Barracks in Warwickshire that they were on their way here and were hiding in Savernake Forest."

"And you have been trying to capture them?"

"They have been able to conceal their whereabouts so far," Major Lawson replied. "But they are very dangerous and a menace to the countryside. In fact their criminal record is the worst of any highwaymen I have ever encountered."

The way he spoke made Vanda give an exclamation of horror.

The Earl bent forward to say,

"Tell me about them please."

"The leader," Major Lawson said, "a man called Baker, who was once a pastry cook. He had a shop in Mayfair and was patronised by the aristocracy, who bankrupted him,"

The Earl looked surprised and the Major explained,

"His clients ran up large bills and eventually, when they did not settle them, he could carry on his business no longer."

The Major paused for a moment to catch his breath.

Then he said,

"As you might imagine, this gave him a grudge against Society and he vowed that he would avenge himself."

"So he took to the road," the Earl exclaimed.

"Exactly," Major Lawson agreed. "He and his gang have not only murdered a great number of people but also tortured them!"

"Oh, no!" Vanda cried out involuntarily.

"I am afraid it is true, Miss Charlton," the Major said. "Baker prefers cash to valuables and so in several instances, having sent out a ransom note to his victim's relatives, if the money is not forthcoming immediately, he has sent them a finger, a toe or an ear, to speed up the payment!"

Vanda drew in her breath and then clutched her fingers together.

She was looking not at the Major but at the Earl and after a moment he said,

"You were so right, Vanda, in making me come here."

"So this is Miss Charlton's doing?" the Major asked. "Then I can assure your Lordship that you are not dealing with storybook 'gentlemen of the road' but a monster and the world will be a better place once he is out of it."

"I can understand that," the Earl remarked.

"Baker and those who follow him have an unpleasant habit when they have taken a prisoner of putting out his eyes so that he cannot identify them."

Aware that what the Major was saying was upsetting Vanda, the Earl suggested,

"You have told me enough, Major, to assure me that I was right in coming to you for protection and Miss Charlton can tell you where the gang are at the moment."

The Major picked up his pen and Vanda said,

"They have left the West wing at Wyn Hall now and were seen by a boy, who told my father's grooms, going into Monk's Wood."

"It is a long time since I was at Wyn Hall," the Major said, "but I think I am right in believing that Monk's Wood is a little South of the house."

"That is right," Vanda said. "It is a large rambling wood and no one in the village will ever go there, which I am sure is why they have chosen it."

She thought that the Major looked rather puzzled and explained,

"Monk's Wood was named a very long time ago after a Priest who left his Priory and settled in the wood to pray and minister to all the animals and birds that came to him when they were injured."

"Now you mention it," Major Lawson said, "I seem to remember hearing the story."

"In the very centre of the wood, which is where I think the gang will be, are the remains of the Chapel he built and where it is said that he administered the Mass not only to any traveller who happened to find his way there, but also to the deer, the foxes, the hares, the rabbits and birds that trusted him to mend their injuries."

"So that is the story," Major Lawson exclaimed. "Then the sooner we can get those fiends out of such a Holy place the better."

"I agree with you," Vanda replied. "I have always loved riding in Monk's Wood because it has an atmosphere that I believe lingers on even though the Monk has been dead for more than two hundred years."

She spoke with a touching sincerity and the Earl smiled at her as if he understood.

"Now, what I suggest," Major Lawson said, "is that his Lordship stays here tonight."

"Tonight?" the Earl asked sharply.

"It is extremely unfortunate," Major Lawson explained, "but at the moment practically every soldier in the Barracks is out on manoeuvres. Some will be returning at about five o'clock today, but the rest will not report in until tomorrow morning."

The Earl's lips tightened, but Vanda, knowing that there was nothing else he could do, said quietly,

"You must stay, my Lord, it would be sheer madness to go back to The Hall now we know what these men are like."

"I agree with you, Miss Charlton," Major Lawson said, "and so I can assure you, my Lord, that we will make you as comfortable as possible. My wife and I will be very honoured if you would stay at our house, which I hope would be more comfortable than the Barracks."

He gave a little laugh before he added,

"All the same you are certainly used to them."

"I am indeed," he replied, "and I was looking forward to being in my own house."

"Of course you were," Major Lawson replied, "but I cannot stress too strongly how dangerous it would be for you to go there alone. I am sure Miss

Charlton is right in thinking that the Baker gang are only waiting for your return."

"Very well," the Earl agreed reluctantly, "I must do as you propose."

"What you and I will do, my Lord," Major Lawson said, "is to work out the best plan of attack, which means, I think, approaching the wood simultaneously from every angle so that there is no chance of any of them being able to escape."

"If it comes as a surprise, it will, I hope, prevent a lot of bloodshed," the Earl commented.

"That is what I will hope," Major Lawson said, "and, my Lord, as you are more experienced than I am in fighting a battle, I shall most certainly bow to your superior judgement in anything we do."

"Thank you, Major," the Earl stated quietly.

There was a little pause.

Then Vanda said,

"I will go home and tell everybody that his Lordship has been delayed in London. The only people who will know that he spent the night at *The Dog and Duck* at Gresbury are my father's grooms, who are absolutely trustworthy."

"If you will do so, Miss Charlton," Major Lawson said, "it would be a very great help and give us a chance to take these felons off their guard."

Vanda rose to her feet.

"My horse is outside and I will leave at once."

Then she hesitated and said to the Earl,

"I had better put your horses into Papa's stable, where no one will see them. If they go to The Hall, your grooms will know that you are not still in London and the highwaymen will get to hear of it too."

"That is very sensible of you," the Earl nodded.

Vanda held out her hand to Major Lawson.

"Goodbye, Major. I can only pray that all this horror will soon be over and his Lordship can enjoy his home-coming in peace and quiet,"

"I promise you, Miss Charlton, that my men will do their very best," Major Lawson answered, "and I shall be looking forward to meeting your father again."

Vanda smiled at him.

Then the Earl rose to his feet,

"I will see Miss Charlton off and then return, Major, to go into our plans in detail."

The Major nodded his agreement and did not leave his desk.

The Earl then escorted Vanda outside to where a soldier was holding *Kingfisher*.

"For God's sake, Vanda," he said in a low voice, "take good care of yourself and don't take any risks."

"No, of course not, my Lord."

She knew that he was thinking of her telling him how she had first become aware of the highwaymen.

He lifted her into the saddle and arranged her skirt neatly over the stirrup.

When he had done so, he looked up at her and their eyes met.

"There is no need for me to tell you that you have been wonderful," he said to her quietly.

"All that matters is that you are safe," Vanda replied.

They were looking into each other's eyes and somehow it was very difficult to look away.

Then with an effort Vanda lifted up the reins and turned *Kingfisher*'s head towards the gate.

She was aware as she went that the Earl was watching her, but she did not look back. She was already praying that he would work out a clever plan with the Major that would put as few men as possible in danger.

She had, however, the most uncomfortable feeling that, if there was going to be a battle with those highwaymen, the Earl would be in the thick of it.

It was quite some distance to the crossroads from the Barracks, but the grooms were there waiting for her.

As she drew nearer, Vanda thought that it would be just impossible to find finer horses anywhere than those that the Earl had recently purchased.

As she drew up beside them, the grooms touched their forelocks and they were obviously pleased to see her.

"These be really fine 'orses, Miss Vanda," one of them said. "We're just 'opin' the Master, when he sees 'em, will be lookin' for somethin' like 'em for our stables."

"We will show them to him," Vanda said, "because we are taking them home with us and not to the stables at The Hall."

The two grooms looked at her in some surprise.

They started to ride off slowly in the direction of the village.

Then Vanda told them all about the highwaymen in the wood and that the Earl was in grave danger.

"That be right terrible news, Miss Vanda," the older of the grooms said.

"I know," Vanda agreed, "and we have to play our part in keeping the secret until the highwaymen are all captured."

She then told them that they had to make everybody in the village believe that the Earl had stayed in London.

So he had not met them as they had expected him to do at Gresbury.

"You set off with four horses and came back with four," Vanda insisted so that the grooms would get the story into their minds, "and unless anyone looks into our stables, they will not have the slightest idea that two of the horses are not the Master's."

"I sees what you mean," the younger groom said. "And we're to tell everyone as asks us that 'is Lordship be still in London."

"That is right," Vanda said in a tone of relief. "And it is very very important that everybody in the village believes you."

"And what about them up at The Hall?" the older groom enquired.

"I will tell Buxton and Mrs. Medway exactly the same tale," Vanda replied.

*

Vanda and the grooms arrived home having been careful not to go through the village.

They had approached The Manor House from the North side so that no one could see the horses.

Vanda gave *Kingfisher* to Jake, who was waiting in the stable yard for them.

Then she went into the house.

Her father, as she expected, was already in his study.

He looked up with a smile when she entered the room.

"You are back, my dear," he said. "I worried when you did not return last night."

"I was afraid that you might, Papa," Vanda replied, "but something very important has happened and I must tell you about it."

She closed the door behind her and pulled off her hat.

Sitting down in front of him, she then told her father the whole story of the highwaymen and how they were now in the West wing of Wyn Hall.

Sir Alexander listened to her in astonishment.

"Why did you not tell me all this before?" he asked.

"Because, Papa, it would have worried you and there was nothing that you could do about their being in the West wing and it was for the same reason that I did not tell Mr. Rushman."

"I think we should both have known," Sir Alexander asserted. "I should have sent to the Barracks immediately."

"They might somehow have flown away," Vanda said quietly. "But now the Earl is in charge and I am sure that they can be captured, which Major Lawson has been trying to do for several months."

"It is absolutely disgraceful that this sort of thing should be happening," Sir Alexander said angrily. "And the Army is so incompetent that they have been unable to bring all these felons to justice!"

This was just the sort of attitude, Vanda thought, that her father would take.

At the same time there had been few soldiers left in the country because of the War.

Also in a County like Wiltshire, where there were so many forests that it was not really difficult for a few men on horseback to be able to hide themselves.

Aloud she said,

"You do understand me, Papa, that no one is to know anything about this except yourself until after tomorrow? I am going up to The Hall now to tell them that you have had a message from London to say that the Earl has been detained, and will be returning later in the week. Somehow I expect the highwaymen will hear of it."

"I blame the Taylors," Sir Alexander stormed, "for being too chicken-hearted to inform anyone in authority what has been going on."

"The Taylors are absolutely terrified," Vanda said, "and now we know what monsters these particular highwaymen are, one cannot really blame them."

Her father was silent and she added,

"You have not told me stories of highwaymen who were cruel enough to put out their victim's eyes or to send fingers and toes to those unfortunates who they were demanding a ransom from!"

"It is not the sort of thing one would tell any child," Sir Alexander replied. "And I really agree with you, my dear, the sooner the Baker gang are hanged at Tyburn the better!"

"That is indeed true, Papa, but you have forgotten that highwaymen are no longer publicly hanged at Tyburn as they were in the past. It was a horrible and barbaric practice with the whole place looking like a fairground with sideshows and street vendors!"

"It was disgraceful," Sir Alexander admitted, "and I do remember as a boy hearing gruesome tales of Society women who waited there as if the place was a Playhouse!"

"Now the gallows have been moved to the courtyard at the Old Bailey," Vanda related. "So the procession and the fairground have been done away with, but the hanging is still open to the public."

"Where criminals are concerned I agree with that as a deterrent," Sir Alexander stipulated firmly.

Vanda picked up her hat and walked towards the door.

It was justice and certainly the Baker gang deserved to die for their crimes.

Yet she did not like to think about any man however bad being hanged by the neck until he was no longer breathing.

After lunching quietly with her father, and they were very careful what they said in front of Dobson, Sir Alexander returned to his study.

It was then that Vanda decided to go to The Hall.

Kingfisher was saddled for her and she entered the Park by the gate that she always used.

Then she trotted under the oak trees towards the lake.

She was thinking constantly of the Earl and she knew how frustrated he must feel having to stay in the Barracks and not being able to return to his home until tomorrow.

She had realised that every instinct in his body rebelled against Major Lawson's decision.

At the same time his brain must be telling him that he would be very foolish to do anything else.

'The Earl is too good a soldier to take any unnecessary risks,' Vanda thought and it comforted her considerably.

She rode up to the front door of Wyn Hall.

Buxton must have seen her approaching for a footman came running down the steps to hold on to *Kingfisher*'s head as another footman helped Vanda to dismount.

It was something that she could easily have done herself.

But she appreciated the fact that Buxton was teaching the footmen the correct way to behave when guests arrived.

He greeted her as she walked straight up the steps to the front door and she said,

"Good afternoon, Buxton. The General has asked me to bring you some news, which I am afraid that you will find disappointing."

"Disappointing, Miss Vanda?" Buxton enquired. "Yes, a messenger did arrive from London to tell my father that his Lordship has been detained, I suspect by the Prime Minister, and he will therefore not come today, as was expected, but as soon as he possibly can."

"Oh, dear," Buxton exclaimed. "Chef'll be disappointed. He's got everythin' ready for a special dinner tonight for his Lordship."

"That is what I expected would happen," Vanda replied, "but naturally, as his Lordship has just returned from France, it is understandable that many important people want to see him as soon as he got home."

"I suppose we'll just have to wait our turn," Buxton said. "I only hopes it's not for long."

"From what his Lordship has written to my father," she replied, "he is as annoyed as you are, but we think in fact he may turn up tomorrow."

"Then that's what we'll look forward to," Buxton said.

As if he wanted Vanda to appreciate the improvements that had been made at The Hall, he said,

"I wonder, Miss Vanda, if you'd just take a look at the silver I've got out of the safe. It's taken a lot of cleanin', but I hopes you'll think it looks like it did when the old Master, God rest his soul, was alive."

"I would love to see it," Vanda exclaimed.

The silver was certainly worth looking at. There were beautiful examples of Lamerie and Paul Storr besides the cutlery, which had all been purchased in the reign of George II.

As Vanda knew, Buxton had a way of cleaning silver that made it shine like a diamond.

As most of the silver was laid out on the pantry table, she looked at each piece with interest.

Afterwards she went upstairs to see Mrs. Medway, who was just as eager to show off as Buxton had been.

Vanda inspected the linen cupboard, where everything had been ironed and rearranged.

It all smelt of lavender which was in bags to be inserted between the sheets and pillowcases.

She was then taken to the Master bedroom, which had always been used by each successive Earl of Wynstock.

The furniture had all been cleaned and polished until it shone as brightly as the mirrors and the silk hangings on the great four-poster bed.

The Wyn Coat of Arms that had been embroidered on the velvet backcloth looked extremely impressive.

There were also spring flowers in vases on the chests of drawers.

Vanda thought that after the years of the War, the Earl would appreciate the comfort, luxury and grandeur of being in his own home.

It was getting rather late in the afternoon when she left The Hall.

She thought that she might talk to the Taylors and then decided that it would be a mistake.

They had kept their word to the highwaymen and had obviously not said anything about them to anyone.

That was just how it should be until the Baker gang were behind bars or hanged.

The shadows were growing longer in the Park as Vanda rode under the trees towards the gate that she had come in by.

She was thinking of the Earl again and she wondered if he was feeling restless at having to stay in the Barracks with the Major and his wife.

Then suddenly and unexpectedly *Kingfisher* reared up.

As he did so, Vanda was aware of a man on horseback directly in front of her.

Then she realised that two other men were closing in on her on either side.

Her hands tightened on the reins as she gave a frightened gasp and the man in front prevented *Kingfisher* from going any further.

Vanda looked at him and saw that he wore a mask.

"If you makes any sound," he said in a common voice, "you'll suffer for it!"

As he spoke, the men on either side of her took the reins from her hands and started to lead *Kingfisher* forward.

Vanda held onto the saddle. At the same time she bit her lip to prevent herself from screaming.

The man in front moved swiftly and the two men holding *Kingfisher* quickened their pace.

They were out of sight of the house and she realised that there was no one to see where they were taking her.

But she herself knew exactly where she was going.

It was only a few minutes before the man ahead passed between the trees at the beginning of Monk's Wood.

As the path narrowed, the men on either side of her fell back.

They did not say a word between them and Vanda lifted up *Kingfisher's* reins, which had been taken from her.

There was no escape with one highwayman just ahead of her and two behind.

She was their prisoner and completely helpless.

CHAPTER SIX

When they had reached the centre of the wood where the little Chapel was situated, she saw a man who could only be Baker.

There was no mistaking that he was in command of the highwaymen.

He was standing there waiting for her as the other three highwaymen were lounging on the grass.

Baker had the air of strong authority about him that she had expected.

She then brought *Kingfisher* to a standstill and he bowed mockingly to her saying,

"Let me welcome you, my Lady, to my humble abode!"

She did not reply.

Baker next made an imperious gesture to one of the other highwaymen to come and take hold of *Kingfisher*.

Vanda suspected that he was going to lift her down, but

she slipped quickly to the ground before he could do so.

"I would suppose," she said in what was an admirably controlled voice, "I need not ask why you have brought me here."

"I imagine," he replied, "you're clever enough to guess that, as the Earl hasn't honoured us with his presence, so you must take his place."

Vanda drew in her breath.

She then could not force herself to ask him the question which trembled on her lips.

Baker was not wearing a mask and she felt that he must have been a decent-looking man when he was attending to his shop in Mayfair, the smartest district in central London.

Now there was something hard and cruel about him and there were several deep lines on his face that she thought did not come from old age but from debauchery.

She did not wish to think about it.

"If you're curious," Baker was saying as the men on the horses moved away and *Kingfisher* followed them, "a note demandin' your ransom has already been left at your father's house."

Speaking in a voice that again did not tremble, Vanda enquired,

"How much have you asked for me?"

"How much d'you think you're worth?" Baker retorted.

He was looking at her in a way that she knew was not only impertinent but also lewd.

She raised her chin higher as she replied,

"I would be interested to find out, Mr. Baker, what you have demanded."

"So you knows my name," he responded quickly. "How might that be?"

"You must be aware that you are extremely famous in the countryside," Vanda replied evasively.

"Too famous!" he said to her harshly. "And if you've told those *damned* soldiers about us, I'll kill you!"

He spoke menacingly and Vanda felt as if her heart had missed a beat.

Then she said,

"I heard a long time ago that the soldiers were searching for you in Savernake Forest, but they could not find you."

Baker threw back his head and laughed.

"We've fooled them!" he boasted. "It's somethin' we'll do again and we won't be hangin' around here once your father pays up."

"I would only hope you have not asked more than he can afford," Vanda replied.

"He can afford for you the same price as those accursed Magistrates have put on my head!"

He spoke violently and Vanda was now feeling really frightened.

Her voice quivered as she asked,

"How – how much is – that?"

"A thousand Jimmy o' Goblins!"

Vanda gave a little gasp and he went on,

"And the longer he takes, the more of you'll be returned to him!"

Vanda knew exactly what he meant and she felt that she must faint at the horror of it.

Then she told herself that the Earl and the soldiers would be here tomorrow.

What she must do is to play for time.

"I suppose, Mr. Baker," she said as she made an effort at self-control, "I should be flattered that my value is the same as yours."

It was impossible for him to miss the sarcastic note in her voice.

He laughed before he said,

"I like your pluck and I hope we won't have to chop too many pieces off you!"

"It is, of course; something you are very good at doing," Vanda retorted. "Do you ever miss your pastry shop?"

Baker stared at her.

"So you know about that too, do you? Well, it's people just like you and that *damned* Earl of yours who can't keep his appointments who cost me my livin'."

"Which I think is very sad." Vanda answered.

"Now don't you start off feelin' sorry for me," Baker snarled. "I enjoy what I'm doin' and, if I have to torture some blasted aristocrats to pay my way, it's what they deserve!"

He spoke in a manner that would have terrified Vanda if she had not known that help would come for her eventually.

She was only praying fervently that what would happen in the meantime would not be too humiliating.

She had hardly looked at Baker's confederates, but she was sure that they were very much rougher and commoner than he was.

There was a neatness about him and he spoke in almost an educated manner. It was very obvious that he came from a better class than any of the highwaymen he led.

She only had a quick glimpse at the men lying on the grass and those who had brought her here into the wood wore masks.

But she knew instinctively that they were all out of the gutter. Or rather the over-populated, filthy and disease ridden slums of London.

They would never have known anything but privation, cruelty and crime.

The men who had brought her to the wood had hobbled the horses so that they could not wander off.

Now they had returned and, seeing that their leader was unmasked, removed theirs.

"What d'you think of 'er?" one of them asked Baker crudely. "Pretty little piece, ain't she? 'Er can keep me warm till the money comes!"

He took a step towards Vanda as he spoke.

Seeing the lustful look in his eyes, she backed hastily away from him.

"Leave her alone," Baker ordered him. "If she belongs to anyone till the cash arrives, it's to me."

Vanda felt that she could breathe again until he went on,

"If it doesn't, you can have your turn later!"

She was so frightened at what he had said that she felt her knees quaking.

"May I sit down?" she asked quickly. "I have been busy today and, as you will appreciate, Mr. Baker, I have missed my tea."

"That's somethin' I can't remedy," he replied, "but you can have a swig of brandy, if you're thirsty."

"No, thank you," Vanda replied.

She now looked towards the ruins of the Chapel. It was behind the grass where the men were lying.

Baker's eyes followed hers.

"That's where we're shuttin' you up for the night," he said harshly, "and if you think you're goin' to escape, you're mistaken."

"I am not so foolish as to try to do so," Vanda answered.

"That reminds me," Baker went on. "I hear your father has some decent horses, which is more than the Earl's got."

"Most of them are getting old," Vanda replied.

"There's nothin' wrong with the one that you're ridin'." Baker remarked. "So I might as well have him as well as the thousand quid your father'll cough up for you."

Vanda wanted to scream.

How could she possibly let *Kingfisher* be taken away from her by such dreadful men like these?

Then she told herself that the Earl and the soldiers from the Barracks would save her and *Kingfisher* as well.

Whatever happened, she must keep her head and knew almost instinctively that if she screamed out or protested they would use it as an excuse to handle her in some way.

It could easily be very roughly and she did not like to think that it might also be something very different.

She was wondering whether she should sit down on the ground.

Then she saw that just by the entrance of what had once been the Chapel there was a fallen tree.

Slowly just in case the highwaymen might think that she was trying to escape, she moved towards it.

Then she turned and sat down facing them.

She held her back straight and her head high.

Baker, who was still standing, was watching her with a smile on his lips.

"You've got class," he said, "as I know, having talked to the beauties of London, as well as the old hags who have been chaperoning them."

"I am only sorry that I did not have the opportunity of patronising your establishment," Vanda pointed out.

"If you had, you'd probably have left your bills unpaid, like all the other rubbish who call themselves the 'Gentry'." Baker said rudely.

"That is not true!" Vanda retorted. "My father always pays what he owes and so do I."

"Then you're the one exception of the rotten crowd who swank about London calling themselves the *'Beau Ton'!*"

He mispronounced the French words, but Vanda knew just what he meant.

"The *Beau Ton!*" he repeated those words furiously and spat. "Man-eating reptiles is what I call them and that's what they are."

Before Vanda could think what to reply, a highwayman came up to Baker.

"'Tis gettin' dark," he said and his hoarse tone sounded as if he had been drinking, "and our stomachs be empty."

"Then light a fire, there'll be no one about to see it at this time of night."

He spoke to the man who was standing beside him, then turned his head towards Vanda.

"That be true, ain't it?" he asked. "There are no spies watchin' us? If there are, then I'll strangle you with me own hands!"

"Why should there be spies watching the wood," Vanda enquired, "when no one comes here for fear of the ghost?"

"Ghost? What ghost?" one of the highwaymen asked.

"The ghost of the Priest who used to live in this Chapel," Vanda replied. "He was a Holy man and the villagers believe that he can be seen at night praying here with the animals who came to him for help – when they were injured."

She spoke very softly.

Not only Baker but also the highwaymen were listening.

"I don' like ghosts," one of them said. "Fair gives me the creeps, they does!"

There was something in the way he was speaking that made Baker say sharply,

"Well, you won't have to stay here for long. Light the fire and let's hope for the lady's sake that her ransom is on her Papa's doorstep at dawn."

Vanda drew in her breath.

She was wondering as the Earl was not coming until late tomorrow, how her father could possibly find as much as one thousand pounds by dawn.

He never kept very much money in the house and Mr. Rushman might perhaps have fifty pounds for staff wages.

She supposed that her father would send his grooms into Trowbridge to wake up the Bank Manager and he could provide the money even if it meant opening the Bank.

When she thought of this, she was sure that the demand for ransom would include the threat that if her father should inform the Magistrates or the soldiers from the Barracks why the money was necessary, she would surely die.

As one of the highwaymen started to light the fire, she wondered if it could be seen outside the wood.

Then she remembered that they had been here for some time and yet no one but herself had the slightest idea that they were in Monk's Wood.

The wood was very thick, with no gamekeepers and the villagers afraid to go into it, that it was totally isolated from all human contact.

Once the fire was burning well the highwaymen erected some posts over it on which Vanda saw they intended to roast a young doe.

They must have killed it in the Park and it had already been gutted and skinned. They set it up in such a professional manner that Vanda then guessed that Baker must have taught them how to do it.

Some of the highwaymen had contributions to make for their dinner.

Large potatoes were set around the fire to cook in the embers and there was a pot that was hung over the flames, which Vanda learned later contained a soup of hare, rabbit and pigeon.

Each man had a tin plate and a mug that he carried in his saddlebag.

They set them down onto the grass and Vanda realised that there was nothing for her.

"Because you're my guest," Baker said in a mocking tone, "I'll share my mug with you."

"I suppose if I was behaving correctly, I should refuse disdainfully," Vanda replied in much the same tone as he had used to her, "but, as it happens, I am extremely hungry."

Baker laughed.

"You've got grit," he said, "and I'll tell you later what else you've got!"

There was an unmistakable innuendo in how he spoke and Vanda felt a streak of fear run through her very like fork lightning.

She recognised only too well that she was walking on a tightrope with these men around her.

It was even more frightening than if she was imprisoned and alone.

The soup was poured into the mugs and was, she had to admit, very palatable.

It was a relief to realise that Baker's mug was clean and she could not say the same of those belonging to the other highwaymen.

And the way they ate made her look away from them in disgust.

As soon as the doe was roasted, they hacked at it with knives, which they produced from their belts and Vanda had a most unpleasant feeling that they were stained with human blood.

They thrust huge pieces into their mouths, spitting out what they did not want and they also talked with their mouths full.

Some of the food trickled down their chins onto their clothes that were already dirty, stained and torn.

It was almost a relief to look at Baker.

He ate as fastidiously as she did herself, his hands were clean and his chin was shaved.

She longed to ask him how he could bear to associate with men who were quite so uncouth and rough.

She could now understand why Major Lawson had said that he only wanted the money and was interested in nothing else.

She knew that what Baker spent his money on would be vastly different from what the other highwaymen desired.

As they finished the soup, each of the highwaymen put his mug upside down on the grass beside him.

Vanda was wondering if it was a custom that had some significant meaning.

Then when they had finished gorging themselves on the doe, she understood.

Baker produced a bottle of rum and it was passed round, each man filling his mug.

"Do you want some?" Baker asked Vanda.

He filled his mug first and also, she noticed, cleaned it out with grass.

She shook her head.

"Have a sip," he urged her, "it'll do you good and warm you. I like my women warm!"

Again she felt the same streak of fear running through her from the way he spoke.

He then turned away from her to pass the bottle on to the other men.

She began to pray frantically both to God and next to her mother.

She called in her heart to the Earl to save her by a miracle from having to stay in the wood for the night with these men.

'Help me – *help me*,' she prayed.

She felt as if her silent plea winged its way towards the Earl like a bird in flight.

She then looked up at the sky.

While they had been eating, the stars had come out and the moon was rising. Already the first of its delicate rays were touching the tops of the trees turning them to silver.

She knew that the moonlight was also illuminating what was left of the ruins of the Chapel behind them.

'Help me – *help me*!' she prayed to the Monk.

Her body was unbelievably tense and she thought even the highwaymen must realise that she was beseeching God, who was greater than them all, to come to her rescue.

The men were drinking the rum and whispering amongst themselves.

She knew that what they were saying concerned her.

If what she feared happened, the only thing she could do was to kill herself.

She was not at all certain, however, just how she could do so.

There was a pistol, and she thought they were loaded, in every man's belt.

They also carried the sharp-pointed knives that they had just used for hacking pieces of flesh from the carcass of the doe.

Would it be possible, she wondered, to get hold of one of those instruments of death?

Then, as the fire began to flicker as it was dying out and the moonbeams became stronger, she knew that it was very late.

Baker poured the last drop of rum that was left in the bottle into his mug and raised it to his lips.

Then he put down his mug and rising to his feet held out his hand to Vanda.

"Now," he said, "you'll come with me and leave these gentlemen to sleep alone."

It was then that Vanda opened her lips to scream.

Even as she did so, there came a sound in the wood, a sound that was so very different from those made by animals moving about in the undergrowth.

And different from the sounds the birds had made in the branches of the trees all the time that they had been eating.

The sound came again and now the highwaymen turned their heads towards the direction that it came from.

*

"Well, we certainly cannot do anything more," Major Lawson said.

"I feel we have considered everything," the Earl agreed.

The two men had planned during the whole afternoon, consulting maps, drawing up plans and thinking out every aspect of a campaign that would ensure that the Baker gang would be unable to escape retribution this time.

"We can only hope," Major Lawson said a dozen times, "that they will not have moved on elsewhere before we can get there."

"If they are waiting to rob me, I think it is unlikely," the Earl replied.

"I can think of no other reason as to why they should have stayed for so long," Major Lawson agreed.

The Major stretched himself as if he felt cramped after having been sitting for so long.

The Earl felt the same.

"We will go to my house," the Major said, "and I am sure, my Lord, you need a drink. I know I do."

The Earl was just about to reply when there was a knock on the door.

The Major had given his orders that they were not to be disturbed.

There was a pause while he collected his papers together and then he called out sharply,

"Come in."

The door opened and a Sergeant-Major marched into the room, clicked his heels together and saluted,

"'B' Company reporting back for duty, sir."

Major Lawson smiled.

"It's good to have you back, Sergeant-Major. I trust our men distinguished themselves?"

"They did indeed, sir, we have received a commendation from those directing the exercise."

"Then I congratulate you," the Earl smiled.

"How many men have returned with you?" the Major wanted to know.

"My Company are all back, sir. The rest should be here in about an hour."

"That is good," Major Lawson said.

He dismissed the Sergeant-Major and turned to the Earl to say,

"I know you will be glad to hear that we can leave first thing tomorrow morning, my Lord."

For a moment the Earl did not speak.

Then, as Major Lawson looked at him in some surprise he said,

"I think it essential that we leave tonight."

"Tonight?" The Major echoed. "But it will be dark and difficult for the men to find their way."

"On the contrary," the Earl said, "there is a full moon tonight and it was a real blessing last night as I only reached Gresbury after darkness had fallen."

"The rest of my men will not be here for another hour," Major Lawson said. "They have been on manoeuvres all day and will be both hungry and tired."

"When he goes into battle," the Earl replied, "a soldier often has to go for several nights without sleep."

The Major flushed.

"I apologise, my Lord," he said. "I realise I spoke like a 'peacetime soldier'."

The Earl took charge.

"This is what I intend to do," he stressed, "and your men must follow me as quickly as possible."

The Earl's trunk had been carried to the Major's house and unpacked by his groom. His evening clothes were laid out on the bed.

It took the Earl four minutes to change from what he was wearing into riding breeches and to put on a grey whipcord jacket.

By the time he came down the stairs the horse that Major Lawson had ordered for him was standing outside the house.

An orderly was holding the bridle.

It was what the Earl had asked for, the fastest horse in the Barracks.

It was not the equal of the horses that he had bought in London, but he knew that it would go faster than those in the team he had borrowed from the General.

Major Lawson did not see him off.

He was busy giving orders and telling the soldiers, who had just assembled on his instructions, what was expected of them.

The Earl set off at a gallop, moving cross-country.

He found his way easily in the remaining daylight and by the time he was near to Little Stock it was dusk and the first evening star had appeared in the sky.

He arrived outside The Manor House and, as he was not expected, there was no groom to take his horse.

He therefore rode into the stables.

An elderly groom appeared to look at him in surprise.

"Why, it's your Lordship!" he then exclaimed as the Earl dismounted. What's 'appened to our 'orses?"

"They will be coming on later," the Earl replied.

He did not say anything more, but walked round to the front door.

He did not knock, but finding it unlocked he opened the door and walked in.

He imagined that, as it was very nearly time for dinner, that Vanda would be downstairs.

He opened the door into what he thought would be the drawing room only to find it empty.

Walking a little further down the passage he opened the door of the General's study.

As he entered he saw the General, whom he recalled, and sitting at a large desk beside him was Mr. Rushman.

Both men had their feet raised on stools and they stared at him in astonishment.

He was about to speak when Sir Alexander exclaimed,

"It is Neil! Thank God you are here, boy."

He spoke so fervently that the Earl asked,

"Why? What has happened?"

"Your Lordship may well ask," Mr. Rushman replied. "Forgive my not getting up, but – "

"Never mind about that," the Earl said quickly. "Where is Vanda?"

"That is what I was just going to tell you," the General answered, "but she told me that you were not coming until tomorrow."

"Where is she?" the Earl repeated.

The General held out a piece of paper.

Even as the Earl took it he had an idea what it contained.

He had not admitted it yet to himself, but he had had a presentiment that Vanda was in danger.

All the time he was riding toward Little Stock he knew that something had occurred that made it imperative for the troops to move in tonight.

On the piece of paper that the General had handed him was written,

"We have taken your daughter prisoner.

If you don't leave one thousand pounds on your doorstep at dawn tomorrow morning, we will then send you one of her fingers, then one of her toes every two hours until the ransom is paid.

Inform no one of this or she will die."

The Earl was completely aware that the note had been written by Baker.

It was in just the same type of handwriting as the pastry maker would have used for rendering his accounts.

"What do you mean to do?" the Earl asked.

"Mr. Rushman and I between us can produce only a little more than fifty pounds," the General replied. "We have sent Hawkins on the fastest horse that is available to the Bank at Trowbridge for the rest."

He looked extremely worried as he went on,

"We can only pray that it will be obtainable from the Manager, although the Bank will be closed."

"At what time do you expect him back?" the Earl asked.

The General made a gesture of total helplessness with his hands.

All three men were aware that Trowbridge was at least seven miles from Little Stock.

There was little likelihood that Hawkins, after arousing the Bank Manager, would be back before midnight.

"We cannot possibly wait for so long," the Earl said. "The soldiers will be coming as soon as possible, but as you are very well aware, General, it takes longer to bring them here by road than to travel cross-country."

There was no need to explain that all the soldiers at the Barracks were foot soldiers.

The General knew that as well as he did.

"What I am going to do," the Earl said quietly, "is to join Vanda!"

Both men stared at him in sheer amazement.

"We all know what these devils are like," the Earl said brusquely. "Even if they don't torture her she is very pretty."

The General clenched his fingers together, but he did not speak.

"Is there a woman in the house?" the Earl asked.

"There is a cook called 'Jennie'," the General replied.

Without making any explanation the Earl then turned to walk across the hall to where he knew that the kitchen would be situated.

Jennie was standing at the stove in the kitchen.

Dobson had brought in the soup tureen and the silver *entrée* dishes and put them on the kitchen table.

They looked around in surprise when the Earl entered.

He then walked towards Jennie.

"I want you to make me a mask," he said, "as quickly as possible."

"A – mask, sir!" Jennie exclaimed.

"My Lord," Dobson corrected her at once.

" – my Lord," Jennie said dropping a curtsey.

"Miss Vanda is in great danger," he explained, "and so there is no time to be lost. Please make me a highwayman's mask."

Jennie gave a little cry of horror.

She pushed the saucepan she was holding to one side, and ran to the dresser where her sewing basket lay.

"Now, where do I have black material?" she asked.

"You've got a black petticoat," Dobson volunteered.

"Fetch it," the Earl ordered. "I will replace it with one far better."

The Earl returned to the study.

"What I intend to do, General," he declared, "is to find Vanda, who is in Monk's Wood with the highwaymen."

Before the General could speak the Earl went on,

"When the troops do arrive, Major Lawson will contact you immediately."

He was about to say something more when he stated,

"I have forgotten something!"

He left the study and ran back to the kitchen.

Dobson had just returned to hand the black petticoat to Jennie.

"Listen," the Earl said to him, "I want two bottles of red wine from your Master's cellar, a bottle of gin and another of brandy."

"We've got all those, my Lord," Dobson replied.

"Then fetch them quickly. Open the bottles, mix all the drinks together and return the mixture to the bottles. Do you understand?"

He paused to say,

"I think I will make it two bottles of brandy."

"Very good, my Lord."

Dobson had also been in the Army at one time in his life and was therefore used to obeying orders without question.

As he hurried to the cellar, the Earl went back into the study.

He told the General briefly what he and Major Lawson had planned during the afternoon.

He explained also that Major Lawson would come first to The Manor House just in case the Earl had learnt anything new.

"What you have to impress upon the Major, General," he said, "is that they move so silently that the highwaymen have no idea they are there until they are surrounded."

"I completely understand, my boy, and I commend you on a splendid idea."

"What I did not expect, and what you will have to tell Major Lawson," the Earl said, "is that Vanda is with them."

Before he could say anything more, Dobson came into the study with the black mask in his hand.

Jennie's needlework was excellent and the slits for the eyes were wide enough for the Earl to see clearly.

The mask covered a great deal of his face and it would be very difficult, even for someone who knew him well, to identify him.

"This is exactly what I have wanted," the Earl said with satisfaction, looking at his reflection in the mirror.

He turned back to the General.

"Wish me luck," he said, "I can only hope that I am in time to prevent Vanda from suffering at the hands of those fiends!"

The General put his hand on his arm.

"God go with you, my boy," he murmured.

Then the Earl was running out of the house and back to the stables to collect his horse.

He then gave the elderly groom, who was startled by his appearance, certain instructions that he had not mentioned to the General.

"Go at once," he ordered.

"I will, my Lord," the groom replied.

He was saddling another horse as the Earl rode away.

Now the moonlight was turning the garden into a scene of exquisite beauty and it seemed impossible there should be such evil lurking in the darkness of Monk's Wood.

The Earl found the path that ended in the Park and led into the centre of the wood.

The moonlight flickering through the branches of the trees cast patterns of silver on the ground ahead of him.

Everything seemed silent, except for the sudden flutter of a bird that had gone to roost.

As the Earl rode on, he began to think despairingly that after all the highwaymen had moved away.

If so, their plan would prove to be useless.

Then in the distance he thought he heard a voice.

A moment later he saw a flickering light and he realised that it came from a fire.

Unless the gang of highwaymen had hurt or imprisoned Vanda, in a few seconds he would find her.

He could only pray that if she recognised him she would not cry out to him to save her.

If she did, it would endanger both their lives and they would both be at the mercy of men who showed none to their enemies.

A minute later he reached the clearing in the centre of the wood.

One glance showed him at once that six highwaymen were seated at a dying fire while the seventh was standing.

Seated on the trunk of a tree behind him was Vanda.

Quickly, because he was afraid that she might shout out, the Earl began,

"Good evening, my brothers. I hope I may join you and it's with the greatest respect that I bow to your leader, Bill Baker."

He rode his horse over the long grass right up to the highwaymen.

He was aware as he did so that several of the men put their hands to the pistols in their belts.

"Who are you?" Baker demanded.

"I am John Garrat, at your service! And naturally a 'gentleman of the road'."

The Earl spoke with such a flourish that one of the men laughed and a second later several others followed him.

"You're certainly well pleased with yourself!" one of them commented rudely.

"But not as pleased as you might be," the Earl replied looking at Baker. "I congratulate you on capturing an heiress. She is, in fact, someone I was looking for myself!"

"An heiress?" Baker exclaimed.

The Earl looked at Baker in astonishment.

"Do you mean to say you don't know?"

"Know what?"

"That she," the Earl said pointing his finger at Vanda, "has a fortune of between ten and fifteen thousand pounds."

"I knew her father was wealthy," Baker said, "but – "

"She has her own money, inherited from her mother," the Earl informed him.

Baker scratched his chin.

"That makes things a bit different. If what you're sayin' is true, I've not asked enough."

"Not asked enough?" the Earl exclaimed incredulously. "What have you demanded?"

"Same as what they put on my head," Baker replied. "A thousand golden Goblins."

The Earl threw up his hands in horror.

"You are cheating yourself! I have a so much better idea than that where an heiress is concerned."

"And what's your idea?" Baker asked.

He was resenting this new man, who he thought looked as smart as he himself did, interfering.

The Earl looked at him through his mask and stroked his chin reflectively.

"Now what would you say," he then asked him in a slow quiet voice, "if I told you how each one of you could make a thousand quid and leave the rest to me?"

"I just don't believe the old Josser could find that kind of money in a thousand days," Baker retorted. "And we're not waitin' that long!"

"No, no, of course not," the Earl agreed scornfully. "I'm leaving at dawn and, if you are not interested in my idea, then I will not press it on you."

"I *am* interested, of course, I'm interested," Baker said irritably. "I just don't believe it's possible."

"Let's 'ear what it is," one of the other men suggested.

There was a chorus from all the others.

"That's right! Let's 'ear what 'e's got to say! 'E might be as smart as 'e looks."

There was a snigger at this and Baker urged,

"Well, come on then, out with it! Tell us just how we can each make a thousand pounds."

"In the same way as Captain James Campbell did."

"Campbell?" Baker repeated reflectively.

"And Sir John Johnson," the Earl prompted.

"Now what did they do?" Baker asked who obviously did not know.

"I'll tell you just what they did," the Earl replied. "They abducted an heiress and Campbell married her!"

CHAPTER SEVEN

Vanda had been so shocked by what Baker had said that she was almost paralysed by fear.

She was now wondering frantically just how she could kill herself.

Suddenly a man rode into the clearing on horseback.

Seeing that he was a highwayman she relapsed into her distraught thoughts.

But, when the Earl began to speak, she stiffened, looked up and thought that she must be dreaming.

She knew his voice, she could never forget it.

But she could not believe that it had come from a man whose face was covered with a black mask.

The Earl went on speaking and she knew that it really was him.

She wanted to jump to her feet, to run to him and beg him to save her.

Every nerve in her body seemed to spring towards him.

Then her brain told her that, if she did anything quite so foolish, she would destroy him.

He was one man among seven dangerous criminals and, if they had the slightest idea that he was deceiving them, he would surely die.

Clenching her hands together, she began to pray that his disguise would not be penetrated.

She realised soon that he was talking as if he wanted to keep the highwaymen interested and she knew that he was afraid that they would move on to somewhere else.

She suspected now that the plans he had made for the soldiers to arrive in the morning had been changed.

Then he spoke of James Campbell and of his marriage to an heiress and she remembered that it was the tale she had told him.

She was aware that he was trying to save her from the highwaymen in a very subtle way.

She heard Baker say,

"I don't believe you can do this."

"I can and I have," the Earl replied.

"Then where's your wife now?"

The Earl gave a little chuckle before he replied.

"Now you are asking *me* questions that I am not going to answer."

Baker laughed.

"You are certainly a cool card," he said, "and we could do with a few thousands, couldn't we, boys?"

There was a murmur of assent from the highwaymen. And they were listening intently to everything that was said, almost as if the Earl had mesmerised them.

He walked to his horse.

"To show you that I am really in earnest," he said, "I have something for you that speaks louder than words."

He drew something from his saddle.

Watching, Vanda saw that it was a small bag of the type Mr. Rushman used when he was paying the wages.

The Earl opened it and tipped its contents into his hand.

They glittered for a moment in the moonlight.

"Catch!" he shouted.

Then dramatically he threw what he held up into the air.

Golden sovereigns soared into the air above the heads of the highwaymen and they fell amongst them.

They scrambled for them like small boys at a fair after sweets.

They snatched up the coins, several men biting them to make sure that they were real.

"This is my Wedding present to you," the Earl said. "Now two of you be off to fetch the Parson."

"And so how do we know for sure," Baker said as the others watched in silence, "that, when you marry the wench, we'll get her money."

"You have to trust me," the Earl replied. "At the same time I will give you my written assurance that each one of you, if alive, will receive one thousand pounds."

"That be fair enough," one of the highwaymen shouted as if he thought that Baker might refuse it.

"You will get nothing if you don't hurry for a Parson," the Earl said. "He lives in the house next to the Church which is only a short way down the road on the left hand side."

Two men then walked towards their horses.

"Make him ride this way," the Earl said. "It will be so much quicker."

"You're certainly very good at givin' out orders," Baker said sarcastically. "How do you know all this?"

"I have been planning to abduct this particular heiress for some time," the Earl replied. "But you came along and queered my pitch."

Baker smiled.

"Too many of us in the same place," the Earl went on. "So I thought we had better join forces."

"There be somethin' in that," Baker answered.

The Earl drew a piece of paper from his pocket.

He walked towards Vanda and sat down on the same fallen tree on where she was sitting.

He did not look at her.

But she felt her whole being vibrating towards him and she was sure that he understood all that she was feeling.

He did not write anything and she wondered just how he could do so without a pen.

Instead, he read to himself what was already written on the paper.

Then he rose and handed it to Baker.

"I guessed that this was what you would want before I came," he admitted.

Holding it up so that it caught the moonlight, Baker read what was written.

"Seems fair enough," he said, "but, I'm still wonderin' how you'll manage it."

"Once the woman is my wife, the Law says her fortune is mine."

Baker nodded.

"And what I then do with it," the Earl added, "is all my business."

Baker was still scrutinising the piece of paper closely as the Earl continued,

"It will be the safest to go to a Bank in London and you must tell me where we can meet, say three or four days from now."

Baker was obviously not keen on going to London.

The two men discussed other places, each having some objection to anything suggested by the other.

Only Vanda knew that the Earl was playing for time and she was listening for sounds of the highwaymen returning.

It was not far to the Vicarage and she was sure that they would hurry there as quickly as possible.

Then, she thought, the Parson, who was an elderly man, would be in bed and fast asleep.

He would have to dress and it would surely be virtually impossible for the Earl to keep Baker talking all that time.

The Earl appeared to come to some arrangement with him and he said,

"Now all we have to do is to wait for the Vicar and that reminds me, I brought you something you can drink to my happiness in."

There was laughter at this from the men who had been listening.

Several made remarks that Vanda did not understand, but she knew that they were crude and vulgar.

The Earl went to the side of his charger.

The horse, which had been well trained, had not moved away, but stood just where he had been left, only bending his head to crop the grass that was in reach.

The Earl pulled the bottles out of the saddlebags.

He carried the first two to Baker, putting them down at his feet.

Then he returned for the other two.

"I may tell you," he said lightly to Baker, "that the wine merchant from whom I procured these was very reluctant to part with them."

He spoke in a way that told the highwaymen that he had taken them at pistol point.

They laughed a great deal and joked about it.

"I could not carry more," the Earl said. "There is more than half a bottle for each of us and we will leave one bottle for the boys who are fetching the Parson."

"They'd 'ave the skin off your back if you 'ad forgot them," one of the highwaymen jibed.

The Earl opened the first bottle and handed it to Baker.

He took a long swig then, as he handed the bottle back to the Earl, he seemed to be gasping for breath.

"In God's name!" he exclaimed when he could speak. "What the hell have you put in the wine – dynamite?"

"The very best French Brandy among other things," the Earl replied, "and there was no duty paid on it either!"

The bottle was now being passed from hand to hand.

The highwaymen had drawn in closer and someone had thrown a few sticks on the fire.

It had made it leap again into flame.

The first bottle was passed around twice before it was empty and Vanda thought in the light of the moon that the men's eyes seemed to glitter.

They smacked their lips after they had drunk. It was as if they relished every drop that had passed down their throats.

The second bottle had been started when Vanda heard the sound of hoofs.

She could hardly believe it that the highwaymen could have been so quick.

A moment later the horses came into the clearing.

The elderly Vicar was riding beside his captors and he was wearing his cassock.

As he dismounted, he lifted down his surplice that had been hung over the front of his saddle.

As if he felt determined to assert his authority, Baker went forward.

"Good evening, Parson," he greeted him. "I see that you have agreed to join a man and a woman we have here in Holy Matrimony."

He was speaking in his usual mocking tone.

The Vicar replied quietly,

"I had no choice, but I am here as you can see."

It was then that the Earl suggested,

"If you stand just inside this old ruined Chapel, you will then be on consecrated ground."

The Vicar did not look at him, but put on his surplice.

Walking past the highwaymen who were now lying on the ground, he reached the Chapel.

The two highwaymen who had escorted the Vicar put their horses with the rest.

Then the others gave them the bottle which had been kept for their return.

The men by now were drinking thirstily.

But Vanda realised that their voices were low. It was as if they were slightly overawed by what was happening.

The Vicar had gone inside what was left of the Chapel.

Part of the Altar was still in its right place, but the roof had fallen in and there was nothing left of the windows.

The Vicar knelt down amongst the broken stones.

The Earl took off his hat.

Then he put out his hand towards Vanda and drew her from the fallen tree.

They stood in front of the Chapel.

As if the Parson was now aware that they were present, he made the sign of the cross and rose to his feet.

First he spoke to Vanda.

"Is it your wish," he then asked her, "that this Wedding should take place?"

"Y-yes."

Her voice was hardly audible and she suddenly felt shy.

It all seemed like a dream yet at the same time her heart was singing.

The Earl was saving her, saving her from Baker and his brutal men and, if she had been capable of it, from having to kill herself.

He was still holding her hand in his tightly and she felt the strength of his fingers.

Although she was desperately frightened that he might be unmasked, she felt a little thrill run through her.

The Vicar then turned to the Earl,

"John is my name," the Earl informed him.

"The Vicar had no Prayer Book with him, but he knew the Marriage Service by heart and he could shorten it if he so wished.

He said a prayer and then turned to the Earl,

"Repeat this after me, 'I, John, take thee, Vanda, to my wedded wife'."

The Earl repeated the words slowly and seriously in his deep voice.

"And finally the Vicar came to, '*till death us do part*'."

Vanda wondered to herself if he thought that this was all a mockery and therefore a sacrilege.

Then she found herself saying very quietly,

"I, Vanda, take thee – John to my – wedded husband."

The Earl pulled off his signet ring and put it on the third finger of her left hand.

He felt her tremble when he touched her, but he knew that it was not with fear.

They both knelt and then the Vicar blessed them.

When he had done so, he then turned back to the Altar and knelt down in front of it as he had before.

While the Service was taking place, all the highwaymen had been quiet.

Now they started shouting,

"Kiss the bride, kiss 'er, or I'll do it for you."

They were all yelling at once, but Vanda could tell that they were slurring their words.

She felt sure that the wine which the Earl had brought them must have been very potent.

She looked at them nervously and then she felt the Earl put his arm around her and drew her close to him.

With his other hand he tipped her head back and his lips found hers.

Because he was aware of just how frightened she was, it was a very gentle kiss.

At the same time she felt as if the moonlight touched her lips and had invaded her breast.

She loved him and, whatever might happen next, as he kissed her she had given him her heart.

For a second the highwaymen were silent and then they shouted out again.

Vanda had no idea what they were saying.

She only felt as if the stars had fallen down from the sky to cover them and she and the Earl were all alone in a world of beauty of their own.

It was then as she gazed at him and the strong moonlight haloed her head, there were sounds of men moving through the trees.

Baker, who was more sober than any of the other men, heard it at the same time as the Earl.

Swiftly he pushed Vanda onto her knees with the fallen tree behind her.

He then placed himself in front of her.

Baker drew the pistol from his waist and fired it into the darkness. His bullet struck a tree.

Another shot rang out, he staggered and then fell to the ground.

Even as he did so, the highwaymen gave out a shout of warning.

Soldiers appeared on all sides of the clearing and they were pointing their guns at the highwaymen.

Befogged and intoxicated by the wine, they were unable even to pull their pistols from their belts.

As the soldiers then converged on them, Major Lawson came towards the Earl.

"We came as quickly as we could, my Lord," he said with a smile.

"At exactly the right moment," the Earl replied, "but I am afraid that you have lost the chief culprit."

Both men looked at the limp body of Baker lying on the ground.

His coat had fallen open and there was already a large crimson stain on his shirt.

"There's a price of one thousand pounds on his head," Major Lawson said, "which, of course, my Lord, belongs to you."

"I suggest," the Earl replied, "that I double it and the money is divided between your men who managed to come here so quickly despite the fact that they have had a long day on manoeuvres."

Major Lawson's eyes were twinkling.

"That is very generous of your Lordship," he said, "and this special manoeuvre here in Monk's Wood will keep them happy for a long time."

He turned from the Earl to shake hands with the Vicar, who was standing in the entrance of the Chapel.

The Earl was suddenly aware that he had not removed his mask.

Now, as he pulled it off his face, he said,

"Thank you, Vicar, you played your part so brilliantly. Miss Charlton and I will talk to you more about it tomorrow. Now I shall take her home."

"I know that the General will be waiting very anxiously to learn what has happened here." the Vicar replied.

The Earl was aware that Vanda was feeling that it was impossible to talk normally to anyone.

He drew her towards the horses.

He lifted her onto *Kingfisher's* back. Then, as if he felt that she was feeling unsteady, he sprang up behind her.

She felt his arm go around her holding her close.

She thought that it was just the most wonderful thing that could have ever happened to her.

The Earl turned *Kingfisher's* head.

As they passed Major Lawson, who was still talking to the Vicar, he said,

"Thank you for the loan of your charger. I will leave it to you to take him back to Barracks."

As Major Lawson saluted, the Earl rode slowly through the wood.

The soldiers and their prisoners in tow had disappeared towards the brakes that had carried them from the Barracks to Monk's Wood.

It did not take the Earl long to reach the gate of the Park that Vanda always used.

To her surprise the Earl pulled *Kingfisher* to a standstill.

And he spoke for the first time since they had left the clearing.

"Are you all right?" he asked her anxiously.

She had been resting her head against his shoulder and now she looked up at him.

"How could – you be so – wonderful as to – save me?" she stammered.

"I ought to be shot for not realising sooner that you were riding into danger," the Earl replied. "How could I suppose that when I did not turn up those scoundrels would turn their attention to you?"

"You saved – me when I was – wondering how I – could kill – myself."

His arm tightened around her.

Then, as if there were no words he could say to reassure her, he bent his head and his lips found hers.

He kissed and went on kissing her until once again she was touching the stars.

Her terror and fear of the highwaymen had now faded away and she was trembling with the wonder of his kiss.

Only when he raised his head did she say in a voice that seemed to come from the stars,

"I – love you, *I love – you!*"

"And I love *you* – but I might have lost you," the Earl answered.

*

Vanda opened her eyes and saw that it was very late in the morning.

It had been so difficult to go to bed last night when there was so much to tell her father and Mr. Rushman, who were waiting for them and becoming increasingly concerned.

She realised just how worried they had both been.

It was only when the Sergeant-Major had returned from manoeuvres that the Earl had suddenly become aware of the terrible danger that Vanda might be in.

It had never crossed his mind for a single moment that she would do anything quite so foolhardy as to ride about the Park alone and at night.

Nor had he anticipated that, because he had postponed his arrival, the highwaymen might take Vanda in his place.

After she had gone and he and Major Lawson were both sitting down to work out their plans of attack, the Major said,

"I, of course, did not say anything at all in front of Miss Charlton, but Baker and his dreadful gang have created the most appalling havoc in some of our small villages nearby."

He saw that the Earl was listening intently and went on,

"There was not very much money to be found there and Baker prefers money to anything else."

He paused before he said,

"Those brutes raped all the young women and murdered any men who tried to prevent them from doing so."

"I am not surprised that you are making every effort to capture Baker, as he is the undoubted ringleader," the Earl had remarked.

They went on working until the Earl suddenly knew, almost as if someone had just told him so, that Vanda was in danger.

He had found her enchanting, amusing and incredibly beautiful.

Perhaps, because they had known each other since she was a child, there was a kind of affinity between them.

It made it possible for him to read her thoughts and to feel in some way, which he did not analyse, that they were a part of each other.

Whilst he was riding as fast as he could towards The Manor House, he remembered the story Vanda had told him of Captain James Campbell and how he had married the girl he abducted.

The Earl was suddenly terrified.

If the soldiers were then delayed for any length of time, Baker might storm the village or The

Manor House and, if he did, either he or his men might rape Vanda.

When he had learnt from the General that Vanda was actually Baker's prisoner, he knew at once that he had to save her or die in the attempt.

As always in the face of the enemy, he appeared cool, calm and in control.

It was almost as if a Power greater than himself directed him.

He had sent the groom to see the Vicar to tell him to be ready when the highwaymen called to collect him.

Then he had left the General to convey his instructions and warning to Major Lawson.

Vanda had learnt last night from her father that it was the Earl, and the Earl only, who had any idea of how he could bring her to safety.

But she was obviously so exhausted that the Earl had insisted that she went up to bed, whilst her father and Mr. Rushman were still asking questions.

He had taken her to the top of the stairs and opened her bedroom door.

Then, pulling her into his arms, he kissed her until she felt as if the whole house was spinning around them.

"Go to bed, my precious," he said. "You are safe and no one will hurt you. We will talk about ourselves tomorrow."

He kissed her again and put her gently through her bed room door and closed it quietly behind her.

She heard him walking down the stairs.

Then the tears filled her eyes and, as she undressed, she was saying over and over again,

'Thank You, God, *thank You*!'

Now the sun was shining brightly and she knew that she was happier than she had ever been in her whole life.

She then dressed quickly, putting on one of her prettiest gowns so that the Earl would admire her.

Next she wondered if she should perhaps have worn her riding habit and gone to meet him at The Hall.

She began to question now in her mind for the very first time if they were actually married.

Was what had happened last night only a pretence to deceive the Highwaymen?

'I love him,' she told herself, 'but at the same time why should he love me when we have seen so little of each other?'

She felt as if she had been wakened from a dream.

A glorious and magical one, but still a dream!

Then there came a sudden blow to her heart.

She recalled that the marriage between Captain James Campbell and the heiress he had abducted had been annulled by Royal Proclamation.

The sunshine seemed to fade into deepening darkness.

She had assumed both that their marriage was legal and that the Earl had kissed her because he loved her.

Any man, she was now thinking, would have kissed her because she was safe.

He was only congratulating himself on being so clever.

The more she thought of it, the more she decided that she had been impulsive and in fact presumptuous.

She walked slowly down the stairs.

It was too late to ask for breakfast and anyway she was not feeling in the least hungry.

The house seemed very quiet, but she was sure that her father would be in the study already.

She next went into the drawing room and the sun was streaming in through the bow window.

Yet she felt as if her world had become suddenly thick with a fog that she could not find her way through.

'What shall I do, what shall I say to him?'

She thought that the most important thing was not to make the Earl feel that he was tied.

She was very sure that there were hundreds of women for him to marry if he wished for a wife.

The stories of all the gaieties of Paris once the War was over had trickled back to England. And she was certain that, because he was so handsome, the Earl had enjoyed them.

'I must make it very clear to him,' she decided, 'that I will not hold him in any way and that, if he wishes to be free, I will agree to anything he suggests.'

*

At The Hall the Earl, who was used to having very little sleep, had awakened at his usual hour.

When he had gone back there last night, he had ridden *Kingfisher,* because the horse was already saddled.

When he had entered his own house for the first time in seven years, the night-footman had hurried to fetch Buxton.

He had jumped out of bed, dressed in a matter of a few minutes and his usual self-composure was unimpaired.

"I deeply regret, my Lord," Buxton said, "that I was not here to welcome your Lordship, but, as you were so late, we were not expecting you until tomorrow."

The Earl held out his hand.

"I am aware of that, Buxton. It is a long story, which you will doubtless hear a thousand times in the future, but I have just helped the Army to capture the Baker gang, who I understand have been hiding in the West wing."

It was impossible not to tell Buxton a little more of the whole saga.

Then Buxton realised that the Earl must be hungry after having had no dinner so the chef was roused and two of the footmen from their beds.

So it was nearly three o'clock before the Earl finally lay down in the bed of his ancestors and fell into a deep sleep.

Now, as he came downstairs, he was thinking of Vanda and decided that he would ride over to see her. He would then return *Kingfisher* and arrange for his own horses to be taken to his own stables.

He was walking towards the breakfast room when he was aware that a post chaise had drawn up outside the front door.

A footman ran down to it and came back with a letter.

One glance at the writing told the Earl who it was from and he carried it into the breakfast room.

He helped himself to the dishes that were waiting on the sideboard.

Buxton had poured out his second cup of coffee before he finally opened Caroline's letter and then he wondered for a moment why Caroline should send it by post chaise.

It was indeed a considerable expense unless there was some urgent reason for it.

He soon learnt the answer.

Caroline informed him that she had arranged a house party at Wyn Hall for the following weekend.

As she had already mentioned, the Prince Regent would be delighted to be his guest.

She continued,

"I hope you will not be angry with me, dearest Neil, but I told the Prince Regent that we were secretly engaged. He has promised not to speak of it to anyone."

For a moment the Earl stared at what she had written, his eyes darkening with anger.

Then unexpectedly he laughed and threw the letter down on the table.

He knew he had found the answer to his own problem when he had solved Vanda's.

Now he was free!

Yesterday in his terror at what might happen to her, he was concerned only with how he could rescue her.

It had never struck him that Caroline was now no longer a menace to his life or his happiness.

He had in point of fact never given her a thought.

Today he was in love and married.

There was no question of his having a house party until he had finished his honeymoon.

He would write to the Prince Regent at once and tell him exactly what had happened.

His Royal Highness would surely be thrilled to be the first in the know.

Although the Earl disliked personal publicity, he knew that it would be impossible for the news of the capture of the Baker gang not to be a sensation and people would be talking about it endlessly for months to come. And the newspapers would be enquiring into every aspect of the story.

He would, whether he liked it or not, become a National hero.

What was more the romance of how he married Vanda in the ruined Chapel would captivate every woman's heart.

Whatever Caroline might say or not say, no one would listen to her.

He rose and went from the breakfast table to his study.

He sent his letter to the Prince Regent at Carlton House in charge of two grooms on fast horses.

Then he mounted *Kingfisher* and rode through the Park to The Manor House. He had always loved his home, but he had forgotten just how beautiful it was.

The sunshine was dazzling.

The spring flowers, the ducklings on the lake and the rooks feeding their young in the treetops, were all telling him that he was starting a new life.

It would be very different from the one he had lived in the recent strenuous and dangerous years.

Having left *Kingfisher* in the stables, he found that the door to The Manor House was open and he walked in.

He had a feeling that Vanda would be in the drawing room.

He was not mistaken and that was where he found her.

She was standing still at the window gazing out at the garden and the sunshine illuminated the exquisite colour of her hair.

For a moment she did not hear him as he walked across the room.

Only, as he reached her, did she turn around.

He thought that the stars were caught in her eyes.

Then quickly her eyelashes flickered and she curtseyed.

"Did you sleep well?" he asked her in his deep voice.

"I was very – tired, as you must – have been too."

"I was also very happy," the Earl said. "You were safe and that was all that really mattered."

Vanda looked away from him.

"I am very – grateful to you for – saving me," she said, "but I am sure that it would – be a mistake for – anyone to – know just how you did it."

"A mistake?" the Earl questioned.

"I am not – thinking only about how you – captured the highwaymen," Vanda said quickly, "but of our – marriage."

She stammered over the words and the colour rose in her cheeks.

"You are ashamed of it?" the Earl asked.

"No – of course not – it is just – that it was a – very clever way of – protecting me, but it was not – legal."

"I don't know why you should be saying that," the Earl replied. "The marriage took place on consecrated ground. My first name is John and, as we are both residents in this Parish, so there was no need for a Special Licence or for the banns to be called."

Vanda drew in her breath.

"But – but you – want to be – free."

The Earl smiled.

"I have not said so."

"You hardly – know me."

"I have known you for, let me think, eighteen years, and before that at least a million years," the

Earl answered, "and I do know something that is more important than time."

"What – is – that?" Vanda asked curiously.

"That you are exactly the wife who I want to take my mother's place in looking after The Hall and, of course, me."

She raised her eyes to his as if she could not believe what she was hearing.

Then he put his arms around her.

"Are you really anxious to get rid of me so quickly?"

"I love – you," Vanda whispered, "but at the same time I am – sure there are many – other women whom you would rather marry – than me."

The Earl laughed very gently.

"Are you really so modest?" he said. "I thought when I saw you, could it really be only the day before yesterday at the inn, that you were the most desirable woman I had ever seen in my life."

"Is that true – really – true?" Vanda asked.

"I swear to you on everything I hold sacred."

He pulled her a little closer and went on,

"I fell in love with you although I was not certain that it was – love until I thought I had – lost you."

"Oh, Neil!"

Their eyes were held by each other's.

Slowly, for there was no hurry, the Earl found her lips.

He then kissed her very gently until the sweetness and innocence of them excited him in a way that he had never been excited before.

His kisses became more insistent and more demanding. Only when they were both breathless did he say,

"If you try to escape from me, I swear I will think out a plan to keep you my prisoner and never set you free."

"That is – exactly what I – want," Vanda murmured.

"I am now a highwayman, my darling one," the Earl said, "and at pistol point I order you to stand and deliver your heart."

"It is – yours," Vanda cried. "It has – always been yours since I – worshipped you – as a child."

"Then go on worshipping me," the Earl said. "I need you and I know that I cannot go on without you."

He kissed her again until they sank down together on the sofa.

Vanda put her head lovingly against the Earl's shoulder.

"What I really came to say," he said, "is that now that you are my wife, l am taking you to The Hall and, as soon as you feel well enough, we will go and inspect the other houses I own, which I have not seen for such a very long time."

"Can – we go – alone?" Vanda asked him.

"We are on our honeymoon, my precious. No one, and I mean no one, is going to interrupt or bother us until we come back to Wyn Hall."

"There is a – great deal for – you to do here."

"I appreciate that," the Earl replied, "but, there is also a great deal for me to learn and discover about my wife and she comes first."

Vanda laughed.

And then she said,

"I am afraid your family will be very – disappointed that you are not marrying – someone more – important than – me."

"On the contrary," the Earl said, "they will be delighted. So many of them admire your father and loved your mother."

He kissed her forehead tenderly before he added,

"What could be better than that you and I should produce exactly the right sort of family to carry on the Earldom?"

Vanda blushed and hid her face against his neck.

"I often – thought," she murmured, "it was sad that you were a – lonely child as – I was."

"We will have a large family," the Earl declared, "and we will turn the West wing into an enormous nursery, so that there will be no highwaymen lurking around at any time to terrify anyone."

Vanda thought of something.

"Taylor said, when he told me about the highwaymen, that they went there to have somewhere to put their haul."

"We will look for it," the Earl said, "but, I think from what Major Lawson said that Baker was not interested in anything but hard cash."

He pulled her a little closer as he said,

"Nevertheless, my precious, if there is anything worth having we will give it to the soldiers and sailors who suffered injuries in the War and who have been left with no pensions."

"I knew you would be upset about that," Vanda sighed.

"It is something I intend to raise in the House of Lords as soon as life returns to normal," the Earl replied.

He kissed her straight little nose before he went on,

"And I am sure, my darling, that you can think of ways of raising money to help the really desperate cases."

"You are so clever," Vanda said, "and you know I will do anything you want. So please, when you are working out plans for this and that, let me help you."

"You will help me, you will be with me and you will love me," the Earl insisted. "That is my plan for the future."

Vanda laughed and put her arm around his neck.

"That makes it so very easy," she said, "because I love you, I love you and I want to go on saying so."

"You cannot say it too often to me."

Then he was kissing her again, kissing her not gently but demandingly.

His kisses grew more insistent and more passionate as he drew Vanda closer and closer.

He knew that he had ignited in her a little of the fire that burnt fiercely within him.

It was very different in every way from what he had felt with any woman before in his life.

She was perfect and she was sacred.

He vowed that he would murder any man who dared to try to spoil her innocence and her purity.

"You are mine – *mine*!" he asserted.

His kisses grew more demanding still, but Vanda was not afraid.

She knew that this was love as it was meant to be.

The merging of two people who were so much a part of each other that they became one united in their love for ever.

'I love you, *I love you*,' she breathed in her heart.

It was a love that would not die, but would grow greater and more glorious month by month and year by year.

It was a love against which they had no defence.

They could only surrender to it totally unconditionally, knowing that it was given to them by God and God alone.

OTHER BOOKS IN THIS SERIES

The Barbara Cartland Eternal Collection is the unique opportunity to collect all five hundred of the timeless beautiful romantic novels written by the world's most celebrated and enduring romantic author.

Named the Eternal Collection because Barbara's inspiring stories of pure love, just the same as love itself, the books will be published on the internet at the rate of four titles per month until all five hundred are available.

The Eternal Collection, classic pure romance available worldwide for all time.

1. Elizabethan Lover
2. The Little Pretender
3. A Ghost in Monte Carlo
4. A Duel of Hearts
5. The Saint and the Sinner
6. The Penniless Peer
7. The Proud Princess
8. The Dare-Devil Duke
9. Diona and a Dalmatian
10. A Shaft of Sunlight
11. Lies for Love
12. Love and Lucia
13. Love and the Loathsome Leopard
14. Beauty or Brains
15. The Temptation of Torilla
16. The Goddess and the Gaiety Girl
17. Fragrant Flower
18. Look, Listen and Love
19. The Duke and the Preacher's Daughter
20. A Kiss For The King
21. The Mysterious Maid-Servant
22. Lucky Logan Finds Love
23. The Wings of Ecstasy
24. Mission to Monte Carlo
25. Revenge of the Heart
26. The Unbreakable Spell
27. Never Laugh at Love
28. Bride to a Brigand
29. Lucifer and the Angel
30. Journey to a Star
31. Solita and the Spies
32. The Chieftain without a Heart
33. No Escape from Love
34. Dollars for the Duke

35. Pure and Untouched
36. Secrets
37. Fire in the Blood
38. Love, Lies and Marriage
39. The Ghost who fell in love
40. Hungry for Love
41. The wild cry of love
42. The blue eyed witch
43. The Punishment of a Vixen
44. The Secret of the Glen
45. Bride to The King
46. For All Eternity
47. A King in Love
48. A Marriage Made in Heaven
49. Who Can Deny Love?
50. Riding to The Moon
51. Wish for Love
52. Dancing on a Rainbow
53. Gypsy Magic
54. Love in the Clouds
55. Count the Stars
56. White Lilac
57. Too Precious to Lose
58. The Devil Defeated
59. An Angel Runs Away
60. The Duchess Disappeared
61. The Pretty Horse-breakers
62. The Prisoner of Love
63. Ola and the Sea Wolf
64. The Castle made for Love
65. A Heart is Stolen
66. The Love Pirate
67. As Eagles Fly
68. The Magic of Love
69. Love Leaves at Midnight
70. A Witch's Spell
71. Love Comes West
72. The Impetuous Duchess
73. A Tangled Web
74. Love Lifts the Curse

75. Saved By A Saint
76. Love is Dangerous
77. The Poor Governess
78. The Peril and the Prince
79. A Very Unusual Wife
80. Say Yes Samantha
81. Punished with love
82. A Royal Rebuke
83. The Husband Hunters
84. Signpost To Love
85. Love Forbidden
86. Gift of the Gods
87. The Outrageous Lady
88. The Slaves of Love
89. The Disgraceful Duke
90. The Unwanted Wedding
91. Lord Ravenscar's Revenge
92. From Hate to Love
93. A Very Naughty Angel
94. The Innocent Imposter
95. A Rebel Princess
96. A Wish Come True
97. Haunted
98. Passions In The Sand
99. Little White Doves of Love
100. A Portrait of Love
101. The Enchanted Waltz
102. Alone and Afraid
103. The Call of the Highlands
104. The Glittering Lights
105. An Angel in Hell
106. Only a Dream
107. A Nightingale Sang
108. Pride and the Poor Princess
109. Stars in my Heart
110. The Fire of Love
111. A Dream from the Night
112. Sweet Enchantress
113. The Kiss of the Devil
114. Fascination in France
115. Love Runs in
116. Lost Enchantment

117. Love is Innocent
118. The Love Trap
119. No Darkness for Love
120. Kiss from a Stranger
121. The Flame Is Love
122. A Touch Of Love
123. The Dangerous Dandy
124. In Love In Lucca
125. The Karma of Love
126. Magic from the Heart
127. Paradise Found
128. Only Love
129. A Duel with Destiny
130. The Heart of the Clan
131. The Ruthless Rake
132. Revenge Is Sweet
133. Fire on the Snow
134. A Revolution of Love
135. Love at the Helm
136. Listen to Love
137. Love Casts out Fear
138. The Devilish Deception
139. Riding in the Sky
140. The Wonderful Dream
141. This Time it's Love
142. The River of Love
143. A Gentleman in Love
144. The Island of Love
145. Miracle for a Madonna
146. The Storms of Love
147. The Prince and the
     Pekingese
148. The Golden Cage
149. Theresa and a Tiger
150. The Goddess of Love
151. Alone in Paris
152. The Earl Rings a Belle
153. The Runaway Heart
154. From Hell to Heaven
155. Love in the Ruins
156. Crowned with Love
157. Love is a Maze
158. Hidden by Love
159. Love Is The Key
160. A Miracle In Music
161. The Race For Love
162. Call of The Heart
163. The Curse of the Clan
164. Saved by Love
165. The Tears of Love
166. Winged Magic
167. Born of Love
168. Love Holds the Cards
169. A Chieftain Finds Love
170. The Horizons of Love
171. The Marquis Wins
172. A Duke in Danger
173. Warned by a Ghost
174. Forced to Marry
175. Sweet Adventure
176. Love is a Gamble
177. Love on the Wind
178. Looking for Love
179. Love is the Enemy
180. The Passion and the
     Flower
181. The Reluctant Bride
182. Safe in Paradise
183. The Temple of Love
184. Love at First Sight
185. The Scots Never Forget
186. The Golden Gondola
187. No Time for Love
188. Love in the Moon
189. A Hazard of Hearts
190. Just Fate
191. The Kiss of Paris
192. Little Tongues of Fire
193. Love under Fire
194. The Magnificent
     Marriage
195. Moon over Eden
196. The Dream and The
     Glory
197. A Victory for Love
198. A Princess in Distress
199. A Gamble with Hearts
200. Love strikes a Devil
201. In the arms of Love
202. Love in the Dark
203. Love Wins